THUG ME THE RIGHT WAY 3

NAI

URBAN AINT DEAD

Contact Author on FB: Authoressnai / IG: @authoressnai / TikTok: @authoressnai / Website: hoodloverssociety.com / Email: hoodloverssociety@gmail.com

Contact Publisher at www.urbanaintdead.com

Email: urbanaintdead@gmail.com

ISBN #: 979-8-9904701-1-8

SOUNDTRACKS

Scan the QR Code below to listen to the Soundtracks/Singles of some of your favorite U.A.D titles:

Don't have Spotify or Apple Music?
No Sweat!
Visit your choice streaming platform and search URBAN AINT DEAD.

Currently on lock serving a bid?
JPay, iHeartRadio, WHATEVER!
We got you covered.

Simply log into your facility's kiosk or tablet, go to music and
search URBAN AINT DEAD.

URBAN AINT DEAD

Like & Follow us on social media:
FB - URBAN AINT DEAD
IG: @urbanaintdead
Tik Tok - @urbanaintdead

SUBMISSIONS

Submit the first three chapters of your completed manuscript to urbanaintdead@gmail.com, subject line: Your book's title. The manuscript must be in a .doc file and sent as an attachment. The document should be in Times New Roman, double-spaced, and in size 12 font. Also, provide your synopsis and full contact information. If sending multiple submissions, they must each be in a separate email. Have a story but no way to submit it electronically? You can still submit to URBAN AINT DEAD. Send in the first three chapters, written or typed, of your completed manuscript to:

URBAN AINT DEAD

P.O Box 448

Maybrook, NY 12543

DO NOT send original manuscript. Must be a duplicate.
Provide your synopsis and a cover letter containing your full contact information.
Thanks for considering URBAN AINT DEAD.

Ant

"Excuse me, can you tell me more about the child they said was missing from the NICU?" I inquired with a nurse who sat at the nurses' station across from our room. She seemed to be preoccupied with everything other than her job as she busied herself with her phone.

"Sir, I can't give you that information. Your doctor will be back to discuss it with you shortly," she responded. By her body language and tone, I could tell she was annoyed by my presence. Little did she know, a nigga was trying to be on his best behavior, but I was about to tweak the fuck out.

"Miss, my daughter was just born a couple hours ago, and she was taken down to the NICU. I just wanna make sure she's safe. You can understand that, right?" I said just as calmly as before.

"Sir, again, I can't give you that information. There's a lot of children in the NICU, and I'm sure their parents are just as worried as you. We still have to wait to get information back from your doctor."

"Bi..."

"Hold on, son." I felt my arm being tugged on from behind. Kris' mother came up on my side, holding Bre's hand. "Lady, if you don't get yo ass on that phone and find my son some information on what's going on in that NICU, I'm gon' hop behind this counter and whip on you so bad, you gon' need the next available bed. I don't wanna show my ass in front of my grandbaby but trust me I will." The lady picked up the phone with a shaky hand and went to do as she was told. "Excuse my language, Bre baby. Here, you hold onto her while I see what information we can get."

"Ma, I'ma bout to lose it. What if someone took the baby? Who the fuck would come in the hospital and take a fucking baby?!"

"I know. We're going to figure it out. Go in there and sit with Kris. She needs you right now, son. The family is on their way now. I sent up a prayer already. God got us. Believe that."

I walked back in the room, and Kris was looking off in a daze. I couldn't take her spiraling again. Sitting Bre down, I turned on the TV to keep her occupied and sat down on the bed next to Kristen. I held her hand in mine and rubbed it.

"He got her, Antwon. I can feel it."

I didn't even want to think about Kane possibly having my child. There was no fucking way he walked out of the hospital with my baby. The more I thought about it, the angrier I got. Jumping up, I went back to the nurses' station.

"Did she say anything, Ma?"

"No, baby. She said they wouldn't give her any information."

Refusing to hear that nobody would give the answers I was looking for, I turned around and took off in the direction of the elevators. Kris' mom followed me, doing her best to keep up with my pace. I kept moving forward, not wanting her to see the tears I shed.

"Antwon, where you going, son?" The elevator dinged, and I stepped on.

Turning around, I quickly wiped my face. "Tell Kris I'll be back. I'm going to find our baby."

She went to speak, and the elevator doors closed. The ride to the NICU floor had my head all fucked up. My heart beat twice as fast in my chest as I fought to combat my negative thoughts of the worst-case scenario. The thought of my child being taken had me seeing red, but more than that, my heart felt heavy. That feeling that I was failing at keeping my family protected was slowly creeping back in my head.

The elevator dinged again, and when the doors opened, I

could see doctors and nurses scrambling. This floor was a stark contrast from where our room was downstairs where everyone seemed to be going about the day as normal. Getting off the elevator, I walked in the direction of the NICU sign. Reaching the door, the *hospital personnel only* sign did nothing to deter my steps as I went to push it open.

"I'm sorry, sir. You can't go in there." I heard a voice say from behind me. Turning, I found an older, Black woman with a warm smile. I was sure my deadly stare wasn't one she expected.

"No disrespect, but I don't give a fuck about this sign or your policy. I'm going up in this motherfucka to make sure my child is in here." I put my hand up against the door and commenced to pushing it open.

"Sir, wait." She placed her hand on top of mine to stop me. "I understand your concern, trust me I do. Allow me to go in and check for you. The last thing you wanna do is be put out of the hospital." I watched her eyes to measure her sincerity as she reasoned with me. Moving to the side, I gave the go ahead for her to check on my behalf.

"Her last name is Phillips." Something about the woman's aura made me trust her a little. She entered the room and left me pondering. The few minutes she left me standing outside the door felt like an eternity. "Lord, I know I don't come before you often, and I might not be one of your most favorite people in the world due to my countless number of sins. Right now, I'm coming asking that you place a hedge of protection around my child. Let no hurt, harm, or danger come to her. In your name I ask for this covering, Amen." Just as I finished the prayer, the nurse walked back out.

"Sir, she's not in there..."

"Nah, don't tell me that. Don't tell me my baby is missing!" I cut her off before she could even continue. My hand curled into a fist, and just before it collided with the wall, she grabbed hold of my shoulder.

"Your daughter is with your wife, sir. Apparently while you were headed up here, another nurse was escorting her downstairs." I tilted my head upward and thanked God for coming through yet again. "She's okay. Here, come on and get in this elevator so you can go lay eyes on that sweet baby of yours." She pressed the elevator for me, and I thanked her. As I went to step inside, she gave a few parting words. "The enemy is out to destroy you, son, but God has other plans." She didn't know just how true those words were for my life right now.

Getting off the elevator for the second time, I hit the corner like Usain Bolt to make it to Kris' hospital room. Looking through the window, I could see she was now sitting up, and the baby was next to her in an incubator. Her mother stood on one side of it in a protective manner, and her dad was on the other side, holding Bre, who appeared to be sleeping.

"My baby ain't going a motherfuckin' place until y'all run those security tapes. What kind of hospital are you running where people can just come in here and impersonate a damn doctor? Y'all got me all the way fucked up."

"Ms. Phillips, we can't begin to tell you how sorry we are. My name is Ben Thomas. I am head of the labor and delivery unit. It is unfortunate that we have to meet under these circumstances. I can assure you that we are going through the security tapes thoroughly to find out who attempted to take your child. We just want to get her back to the NICU, so we can monitor her." There were two other doctors with him who remained silent the whole time he spoke.

"Attempted kidnapping. Abduction." I made my presence known, pushing through the door. "Let's call it what it is. As far as I'm concerned, y'all failed to keep my fucking child safe in the first place, so back in your care will be the last place she'll be going. I would ask why there hasn't been not one single cop in here to question us since it was determined that a child was missing. MY FUCKING CHILD AT THAT!" I barked, making the doctor jump a little. "At this point, there's no need. Start the transfer papers and get those tapes to my lawyer like yesterday. You might want to get a pen and paper and write this down."

Doing as I asked, they scrambled past me and out the door. I didn't have time for small talk, and if I had to arrange for transport for Kris and my baby, I would.

"Hey, we got here as soon as we could," Kaia said, running in with Maine and Heaven behind her. "Ooh, let me see her. Why she in here and not in the NICU?" They all looked to me and Kris with questioning eyes.

"You gotta be fucking kidding me. Almost kidnapped? What the fuck is going on?! Excuse my French, auntie." Heaven was the first to react after I explained the last few hours we had.

Kris sighed before responding. "All I know is that someone went into the NICU dressed as a doctor and got as far as the freight elevator with the baby. According to one of the doctors, the only nurse who seemed to be doing her damn job noticed an unfamiliar face, and when she called out to the person, they got spooked and took off toward the stairs, leaving the baby there." We all looked at each other, already knowing who the culprit was without having to speak his name.

Seeing my newest baby girl hooked up to a breathing apparatus and wires taped to her little chest crushed me. Maine hadn't said a word since he walked in. He just watched. Making eye contact with him, he gestured for me to step out into the hallway.

"Yo, I don't know about you, but I'm done playing cat and mouse with this dude. We all know that it's him that came up in here. This shit ain't no coincidence. How he even know y'all was in here?" Maine was saying what I already knew and what had already crossed my mind.

"He gotta have ties to someone that's around us often and familiar with the moves we make. I know for a fact it ain't

Chloe because I all but banned her from having any communication with Bre since the last dummy move she pulled."

"You still in touch with his old partner?"

A lightbulb went off in my head. I hadn't even thought about that.

"I cut him off the same time I did Kane. So, nah, I haven't been in contact with him, but now, I have a reason to be. I don't know how willing he'll be to talk, but at this point, anybody can feel this heat that's not tryna be cooperative."

"Aye, I need to talk to y'all," Kris' dad said as he walked out of the hospital room. "I'm going down to the café to get my wife some tea. Y'all take a walk with me."

I hadn't heard from Mase much since we'd been going through our series of unfortunate events. I didn't know his take on how I was moving, and as a man, whatever he wanted to talk to us about and however it came out at this point, I knew me and Maine would have to take it on the chin. At the end of the day, Kristen and Kaia were his daughters long before we became their men. He was their protector as well.

"Aight." We fell in step behind him and walked in silence down to the café. Turning the corner, Mase stopped to face us.

"When we put our girls in your hands, we did so under the pretense that no harm would come to them. Now that the two of you have created your own families, you do understand the issue that I take as a father when I see my children hurt, yes?" Maine and I both nodded. "Cool. That said, I'm gonna need in on any moves y'all make going forward. Now, I may not be a street nigga, but I am a father that's willing to do whatever to ensure the safety of my girls." He gave us both a look that I quickly decoded without him having to say anything else.

Like us, Mase, too, was willing to lay everything on the line in the name of family. Waiting for Kane to come out of the shadows and get at me on some man-to-man shit backfired, and now, we were on the hunt again.

Kane

"Fuckk!" I yelled out, throwing my glass up against the wall, missing Chloe's head by an inch as she walked out of the bathroom. She flinched and ran back inside, making sure to lock the door behind her. That was the best place for her to be at the moment because I was drunk and liable to do her like I had done China. It had been less than twenty-four hours since I tried to kidnap my daughter from the hospital where she was set up in the NICU. I would've gotten away with it too had it not been for a nosey ass nurse who wanted to play hero.

The fact that I was able to get into the personnel room with my doctor's get up that I purchased at a costume store shocked even me. Had I not been on a mission trying to take my kid, I sure would've had the director of the hospital's head for their lack of security procedure. What made it worse was how easy it was to swipe a badge off one of the NICU nurses as they walked out of the room just by bumping into him. I was so close to getting the baby, I could taste it, and then, the feeling was just gone.

"Chloe, bring yo ass out here now!"

I heard the lock on the bathroom door click, and I sat down to pour myself another drink. She walked out and stood at the door, avoiding my eyes. We had been holed up in a hotel not too far out from the city, keeping a low profile. After what happened with China, I knew I had to stay lowkey. I didn't want to be alone, and it didn't take much convincing to get Chloe to accompany me.

China's mom had been blowing up my phone, looking for her, and I kept all my answers short regarding her whereabouts. I was starting to run out of things to say, and as of yesterday, I stopped answering her calls, opting to text instead. I'd gone so far as to send her a message from a text free number, pretending to be China, citing that she was overwhelmed and needed a break from me and the baby. I needed to do something to allow me some time to think. She loved Kristine so much that she was more than happy to keep her until China returned. Unfortunately for her, there was no rising from the dead.

"Yes?" I snapped back, hearing Chloe's voice. She was still

staring past me. Understandably so, I was losing it in front of her.

"Here, come have a drink with me." I poured her a shot of Don Julio and slid the glass in the direction where she now stood in front of the little table set up in the kitchenette.

"No, thank you. I'm fine."

"I insist." Nodding toward the cup, I let her know that she had no choice but to indulge. I paid attention as she took a baby sip of the high-priced tequila. "I need you to do me a favor." What I was about to ask would be received with a lot of hesitation on her end, but I was fresh out of options. If I played my cards right after this next move, I was almost positive that Kris would willingly come to me with my baby. "I need you to go back and make nice with Ant. Get your daughter back and bring her here."

"What do you mean bring her here? What does my daughter have to do with any of this? You said that we were leaving her out of it. You and I both know that Ant won't allow me to be alone with her. Especially after the last time we spoke." I stood, and she flinched. Leaning within an inch of her face, I grabbed her chin and squeezed it.

"You need to come up with something believable and quick. Your baby father has his hands full playing daddy to his own daughter; I don't need him getting too close to mine. When he finds out that I have Bre, he won't second guess parting with Kristen and my baby. Now, get yourself together so I can take you back to your apartment. I have something I need to handle."

I let her face go, and she got up to do what I instructed. Returning back to my seat, I scooped up the powdery substance on the table with the hotel keycard and set it up in a straight line. Using a rolled dollar bill, I took a big whiff, and the cocaine settled me in the way I needed. I dabbled in the drug here and there after Kristen left me but for recreational use only.

Since the accident with China, I started back up, and now it was becoming a full-blown habit. It didn't matter that the coke made me more violent. I wasn't changing anything until I got Kristen. Once she and my baby were here with me, I would stop everything cold turkey. Well, after I rid the both of us of Ant. Taking another hit, I threw my head back so that my nose wouldn't drip, causing me to lose the high I so desperately desired.

"What happened to you?" Chloe questioned. Her voice held pity and a bit of disgust.

"I'm fine," I replied while straightening my button up shirt that I wore for my doctor disguise.

"You're not fine, Kane, and I'm really worried about you." She bent down in front of me and reached for my hand. "You need help, baby. This shit is getting the best of you. You're not the same person I met." Like she actually gave a fuck. "Despite how you do me sometimes, I really care about you."

"I said I'm good. Now come on so we can go. You're

starting to sound like China." I pulled back from her and stood up.

"Where is China?"

"Gone." My answer was flat and emotionless.

Pushing past her, I reached for my gym bag on the floor. Changing out of the button up, I threw on a t-shirt, put on a hat that covered my eyes, and we left the room. Paranoid that Chloe may try to escape me, I led her out of the hotel with my hand on the small of her back. The drive to her house was silent as far as words spoken between the two of us, but the thoughts in my head were having a conversation of their own. *You should let this go and turn yourself in to the police. You know you're only taking those drugs to mask your guilty conscience. Seek help and everything else will fall into place.* Shaking my head wildly, I swiped my hand down my face.

"Are you okay?" I heard Chloe ask, but her voice sounded far away. "Kane!" she screamed, and my eyes shot in her direction.

"What the hell are you yelling for?!" I snapped.

"You're sweating, and I asked if you were okay."

"I'm fine, damn. Are you okay? You keep asking me that shit."

"Forget it. I won't be concerned with your ass anymore. You know, out of the women you claim to love so much, remember it's me you keep around. Correction, I'm the only one that you can have that you seem to keep around. I haven't heard a peep out of China. God only knows where she is. And Kristen has and will always be out of reach."

I was too high to deal with Chloe right now. She and I both knew how severe a beating could be with me in this state. Arriving in front of her building, she gave me one last look of sympathy and got out. She seemed to be hesitant about completing the task I'd set for her, so I wanted a fall-back plan in case things didn't work out in my favor again.

Once Chloe was in her building, I drove my car in the direction of my old partner's house. Ross was my partner from the department who put me in touch with Ant in the first place. He was as dirty as they came, so I wasn't surprised that he was on someone's payroll. Prior to me getting down with Ant, I could recall doing unsanctioned raids with Ross where we got away with beating dealers' asses and taking their money. It was a rush that I surely missed. Getting put on with Ant ensured that we had consistent money, and we didn't have to work as hard.

Pulling down my visor, I checked my appearance, and I looked worn out. My eyes were red, and the bags under them gave away the fact that I was barely getting any sleep without me having to verbalize it. Reaching inside the glove compartment, I fished around for the Visine I kept for times like this. Ross would call me out immediately if I showed up at his home looking high out of my mind. Readjusting my hat over my eyes, I got out and jogged up the steps of his brownstone. I didn't know what to expect when I showed up, which was why I didn't call. I wanted to look him in the face when I made my request. Ringing the doorbell, I shook off the high that I was coming down from.

"Who is it?" A woman's voice, that didn't belong to his wife, answered. As I went to reply, I heard Ross' voice scolding her from behind the door.

"If you don't get yo' ass from in front of my door. Do you pay bills here? No, you don't, so don't answer my shit. Who is it?"

"It's me, Kane. Open the door. It ain't summertime out here." I heard the locks pop, and when he cracked it open, he didn't greet me with a brotherly hug or smile like I was expecting. "Wassup, man?"

"Nigga, don't wassup me. What you doing here?"

"Who pissed in your cornflakes today?"

"Man, don't nobody eat that cheap ass cereal. I wanna know why you at my door after you made us lose out on all that damn money with Ant? Yo' ass went rogue and didn't tell me shit."

"That's kind of why I'm here. Can I come in? Or we gonna continue talking through the door?" He paused for a second before opening the door enough for me to step inside.

"Who was that chick that answered the door?" I asked in case I had missed something. Ross was married with three kids. The woman at the door wasn't his wife.

"My business, mind yours. Look, you have a bounty on your head right now. I shouldn't even be talking to you. The only reason I let you in is because I wanna hear this dumbass explanation."

"Kristen." That was the explanation I had and all I felt I needed.

"Come again."

"Kristen is my reason." Ross knew about my relationship with Kristen before the demise of it. He also knew that my feelings had never wavered for her even while I was with China.

"You mean to tell me that you fucked up the money over your ex? Nah, that's not what you telling me right now. Hell nah!"

"Look, Ant disrespected me, and now he has two things that belong to me. There's no getting around the issue he and I have. I didn't mean for that to fuck up your money, but that says a lot about what he thought about you in the first place."

"And how has this shit worked out for you thus far?" he countered. "Exactly. You're jobless, and you no longer have a side hustle. You said fuck me in the process, and what's even worse is that you kept me in the dark about the shit. The only plus side for me is that I'm still employed. Make it make sense to me, man."

"I have some money I put to the side. Don't worry about that. I'm here because I need your help." He gave me a skeptical look but didn't speak, so I continued. "I need you to plant something on Ant that sticks, so I can get to Kristen and my baby."

"Oh, you must have went from doing coke to smoking dust. No way in hell am I going on that dummy mission; you can count me out. Plus, Cap has been on our ass since the house is being investigated. No can do, brother."

"I know you, Ross. You ain't never been by the book since I've met you. You're scared, and I never thought I'd see the day when you'd be scared of anyone. It's cool though. I'll do this shit on my own."

"Good luck with that. Just remember being scared and being cautious are two different things. Acting on emotion is a sure way to get you killed."

"As long as someone is going with me, I'm willing to take that chance." With no ally in Ross, I was back to square one — me. I got back in my car, pissed that my so-called friend was hanging me out to dry. Pulling out my small baggie of coke, I stuck my finger in it. I needed another hit. Before I could get it to my nose, my phone rang. Looking over in the middle console, I saw China's mom's number pop up.

"Damn, lady, give it up," I said to myself. I snorted the coke from my pinky and answered the phone. **"Hello."**

"Hi, Kane, it's Doris."

"I know, Ms. Doris. I have caller I.D."

"Right. I'm calling to find out if you've heard anything from China yet. I've never gone this long without speaking to her. I'm worried."

I sighed, closing my eyes. **"I hear you, Ms. Doris, but no, I haven't heard from her either. When I do, I'll be sure to** let you know." I wanted to get her off my line so that I could enjoy this high.

"**Well, I'm going to go head and file a missing person's report. She has a child, and my spirit is telling me that something is terribly wrong. Even the text she sent me about needing a break seemed off.**"

That statement sobered me real quick. The last few times we spoke, she had mentioned going to the police, and I was able to talk her out of it. This time, she sounded like she meant business.

"**Umm, let me do some more looking. You know I have some detective friends that can help. I don't want you to get all worked up. I promise I'll get us some answers.**"

"**Okay, Kane, you do what you have to do. And by the way, your daughter is fine.**" I knew that was a dig. I was losing control, and I didn't like that feeling at all.

CHAPTER 3

Kristen

I hadn't been Mackenzie's mother a full three weeks, and I was beyond in love with my little girl. Any negative thoughts I had about my ability to be a mother took a back seat the moment the doctor mentioned a missing kid. I knew instantly that my baby was the one missing. Kane was causing me so much fucking grief. When he was finally put in the grave, I was sure to two step on it in celebration. I cursed the day I met him.

While at the new hospital we were transferred to, both Ant and I stayed on the doctors and nurses like hawks. We practically stood guard at the NICU day in and day out to ensure our child's safety. We'd found out that she was indeed a Brown baby, and today was the day we were taking her home. According to her doctor, she had gained a good amount of weight for release, and I couldn't be happier.

"Babe," Ant called out to me as I dressed Kenzie in her second outfit of the day.

"Yes, love?"

"I love you," he professed. The heavy emotion behind his words made me turn around once I snapped the final button on Kenzie's onesie. Walking over to where he sat on the bed, I pulled his face to mine and pecked his lips twice.

"I love you more. Is everything okay?"

"Nah, but it will be. Is she ready? I wanna get her home." I nodded, deciding not to use the moment to elaborate on the words he'd spoken.

A knock at the door pulled both our attention. I gave the person on the other end the okay to come inside.

"Ahh, man, y'all was really gon' sneak out and not pass by the NICU, so I could say bye to the diva baby." One of the nurses that doted on Kenzie during our stay peeked in the room before pushing the door open. I'd become a familiar face on the NICU floor and bonded with a few of the nurses. Me and Nurse Kat were the closest. She had given Kenzie the nickname of "diva baby" because Kenzie would cry if she wasn't swaddled a certain way, and Nurse Kat had it down to a science, teaching me in the process.

I laughed and waved her over. "No, I was gonna do a little walk through, but since you're here, you saved me a trip." She walked over to hug me and gave Ant a pat on the back. I put Kenzie in her arms, so she could say her goodbyes.

"You guys are so lucky. This baby right here was meant to be. Now remember, Mackenzie, try not to give Mommy and Daddy too much trouble in the middle of the night. Remember Nurse Kat taught you to respect other's sleep." Ant chuckled and so did I as she talked to Kenzie like she was grown before handing her back to me. "Y'all have a safe trip home and thank you for sharing her with us."

"Thank you for taking care of her as if she were your own. And I will be using your number in case she forgets that respect thing."

"Anytime, girl." With one final hug, she left out.

I checked the room once more to make sure we weren't leaving anything behind, and then, we made our exit.

"Baby, call your mom and tell her to meet us at the house with Bre. I miss my little mamas." During our stay at the hospital, I watched as Bre admired the baby from afar. There were even times when the nurses would let us sneak her into the NICU for a few minutes to visit with her sister. I knew that with Ant's schedule, there would be some challenges taking care of two kids, but I would adjust. I didn't want Bre to feel left out in any way, so she would be home with us too.

"Aight. I'll give her a call once we get settled."

I sat in the back with Kenzie, ensuring a smooth ride for the both of us. This first-time mommy thing had me on edge about everything. And the way I was feeling, I was ready to ride in the back with my baby until she was ready for a booster seat.

"Is there anything about Kane that I need to know that may help me track him down?" Ant inquired out of nowhere while looking back at me through the rearview mirror. The question kind of threw me off, not because I didn't want to give him information but because I wasn't expecting it.

"Umm, not really. He doesn't have much family. I know he had a falling out some years ago with his father, and they've been estranged. Mother has been in the wind all his life to my knowledge. The grandmother that raised him passed away some time ago, so yeah, no real family." I wasn't sure if my answer helped at all, but there wasn't much to Kane. "Oh, wait, he has a cousin too, but I never met her before. According to him, it had been a little bit since they spoke as well. Here, hand me my phone from my bag. I can call China and see if she has any info. Or you can call ya baby mama." I snuck the last part in there.

"I don't trust her or Chloe. And I'm still pissed about you going behind my back tryna seek your own revenge. What if you would've gotten close enough and that nigga decided that he could do without you, then what?"

We'd had this conversation about me plotting, and it was clear that he was still harboring some ill feelings about it even after he told me he understood. In hindsight, I saw how me moving on my own accord could've been catastrophic, but all I could think about was revenge. Plus, as soon as I was able to execute my plan, I was going to handle China. Ant and Kenzie's unexpected arrival put a halt to all of that.

"I understand, bae. I don't trust China either. At the same time, she's the closest thing to him. If I stay in touch with her, I — I mean you — have a better chance of getting to him."

"Yeah, aight." He handed me my phone and focused back on the road.

Dialing her number, the call went straight to voicemail. I tried again and got the same result, indicating it was either dead or turned off. Something was wrong because usually when I called and she didn't answer, it was because Kane was around. In that case, she would send me a message to let me know. The last time we spoke, we were supposed to meet up, but she never showed. I was curious as to why but didn't press the issue. I knew she was playing with fire and had to be cautious. Figuring she'd reach out again soon, I didn't call again.

Finally arriving home, Ant grabbed the car seat while I took the baby bag. I couldn't wait to lay in my own bed and get a good night's rest. Being that I was on my anti-baby shit, I hadn't let Ant set up a baby room for Kenzie. I was regretting it now. As he walked ahead of me, I thought about all the stuff I planned to order. Sticking his key in the door, Ant pushed it open, and we were greeted by a welcome home banner and all of our family.

"We didn't shout surprise because we know how that

worked out the last time," Heaven joked while taking the baby bag from my shoulder and kissing my cheek.

"Shut up." I laughed, smiling big as everyone stepped forward and fawned over Kenzie, whose car seat was now propped up on the coffee table in the living room.

"Alright, everybody line up and come get this hand sanitizer," I heard Ma Jane yell from the back, making everybody crack up laughing. "A he he hell, y'all not about to give my new grand the cooties. So come on and get to cleaning."

"I know that's right," my mother cosigned, closing the door behind me.

As they lined up to do as Ma Jane demanded, I made my way to Ant, who stood off to the side with a smirk on his face.

"You think you so slick, huh?"

He nodded before responding. "Ahh, a lil' sum'n. Wait till you see what else they did."

He didn't give me a chance to question him before he walked away to join everyone. Between his family and mine, I could always count on them to be up to something. The welcome home party lasted just two hours, and I was thankful that everyone understood that mama needed her rest. Being around our people further proved how much our village meant to the raising of our children.

"Okay, sissy, good luck on your first night home. Now, if you need me, don't hesitate to call me. I'm like super mom around here," Kaia boasted with Kymani on her arm.

"Girl, go head. You been a mommy for two seconds, and

now you're an expert." My mom laughed, and we both joined in. "On a serious note though, I am so proud of you girls. You both have men that love you so much and have now created families of your own. With all this turmoil that has transpired, I'm happy to be in this moment. Now, Kaia, you're approaching the end of your gap year, so I need you to start looking into getting back in the books, boo."

"I'm already on it, Mommy. Thank you for respecting my decision and accepting Maine. He has been helping me apply to colleges as well, so before you know it, I'll be out of the house and out of your hair."

"Chile, you're barely there as it is. I'm happy to hear that Maine is supporting you though. Kristen, you do whatever you have to do to keep this baby safe from that unstable bastard, Kane. And when I say whatever, I mean whatever." She winked her eye at me and walked off. I was definitely picking up what she was putting down.

"Alright, baby girl." My dad came up and kissed my forehead. "I love you, and I'm happy y'all are home."

"Thanks, Pops. I love you too. I'm gonna call y'all in the morning."

"Not if ya mama don't call you first."

My mother pinched him, and he laughed, pulling her by her waist to the door to leave.

"Hey, I wanted to run something by you," Kaia said after making sure my mom was out of ear shot. She readjusted Kymani's little chunky self on her waist before continuing.

"Has Ant mentioned anything about Simone and Maine?" My brow raised, trying to figure out where she was going with the question before she got there.

"Anything like what?"

"Like is the bitch still sniffing around my man." Her neck rolled along with her eyes.

"Oh, no. I thought you had a conversation with her about that already."

"I did, and Maine is aware of it as well. Still, I don't trust her. And you know I'm far from the jealous type, Kristen, but there's that feeling. And it's not that I don't trust Maine, but that sneaky bitch there... I'm ready to tell that hoe to meet me in the field wit it."

"You know I get it. I haven't heard anything, but I'll be sure to keep my ears wide open."

"No, you don't understand. I need you to be Dumbo around this bitch." I tried to remain serious but couldn't help but to crack up laughing at her animation as she moved her head from side to side.

"I got you, sister. Come here, Mani. Auntie miss you." I made baby noises with my niece, and she got a kick out of me.

"Feels good to be home, right?"

"Yes. Feels even better not to have to sleep with one eye open or have to stand posted up at the NICU, on edge, waiting for something to happen."

Kaia reached out and rubbed my arm. "I know, sissy.

You home now though, and our village has y'all covered. Call me tomorrow so we can start talkin' playdates."

"Kaia, please, okay. I ain't scheduling no playdate. I'm BIG auntie. I'm poppin' the fuck up. I love y'all."

She giggled while making her exit. "Love ya more!"

LATER THAT NIGHT, I snuggled up with Ant, Bre, and Kenzie on the couch, and my body felt settled for the first time in days. Even though my body was at peace, my mind still drifted to thoughts of Kane and what he had up his sleeve. I knew for a fact that he was somewhere in the shadows, still plotting on our demise. And now that Kenzie was here, I knew there were no lengths he wasn't willing to go to get to us.

"Kris?" Bre called out to me, pulling my eyes from Kenzie, who was sleeping so peacefully on her daddy's chest. She was in between both Ant and I as we watched *Moana* for the ten thousandth time.

"Yes, pretty girl?"

"Are you my mommy too since Kenzie my sister?" Her eyes never left the TV screen when she asked, and when I went to answer, I froze. I turned my head to Ant, and he was staring dead at me as if he was waiting for me to answer as well.

"Umm, help me out here," I whispered to him, only for him to smirk and shrug his shoulders.

"She asked you, not me." I pinched him and focused my attention back to Bre. Pausing the TV, her eyes shifted in my direction with a confused expression.

"So, about your question, pretty girl. You have a mommy, but I would love to be your bonus mommy." She still looked confused, so I explained. "A bonus mommy is like a second mommy that loves you very much and will buy you anything you ask for as long as you're good."

"Oh, okay. I like that."

"Yeah, I bet you do, you little con artist," Ant said with his eyes closed and a smirk on his face. I snickered and un-paused the TV. I was here to be whoever Bre needed me to be because, at this point, we couldn't count on her mama to be shit but a puppet for Kane.

"Hey." I tapped him, and he turned his head to look at me. "Thank you for always showing up. Our family being here to greet us earlier, you facilitating the room makeover for the baby, and this moment right here is just a testament of your endless love for me. With so much bs going on, you've reassured me time and time again by your actions that you got us." Feeling myself getting misty eyed, I wiped my face quickly before Bre could turn back and see me.

Taking my hand, he put it up to his lips, kissing my palm. "There's no limit to how far I'm willing to go to see to it that y'all are safe and most of all happy. I'm gon' always have us.

Even when it look like we trippin', we ain't never gon' fall, Kristen. I'll bet the house on that."

The tears won the battle as they trickled down my face. "I can't wait till this six-week hiatus is up. I swear I'ma let you do me so n-a-s-t-y." I spelled the words to protect Bre's ears.

"You won't have to wait. I'm punishing something in the second week." He blew a kiss at me and closed his eyes.

There was no telling how long this peace was going to last, but I wanted to sit in it for as long as I could.

Chloe

I hadn't seen or spoken to my daughter in a minute, and I couldn't understand how Ant could be so cruel. I would never do anything to put my child in danger, and anyone that knew me would attest to that. From the outside looking in, my actions may have shown differently lately, but I was a damn good mother, and Ant wasn't going to take that from me based on the current circumstances. My relationship with Kane was something that I couldn't put into words, and that wasn't a good thing. My track record with men was terrible, and I thought I'd lucked up with Kane. I thought dating him would help me finally get over Antwon, and he did at first.

He did all the right things, charming me right into his arms. When we first met, Kane was the perfect gentleman. He expressed how he loved kids and gave me genuine compliments every five minutes. In the beginning, he was a breath of fresh air, and his presence in my life made me change the way I acted toward Ant in a positive way. Boy, how that shit changed once he found out Ant was Bre's father. It was like a switch in his head went off, and he changed up on me. Our daily conversations, that were once all about us getting to know each other better, seemed to somehow turn into him bringing up Ant.

He'd ask things like how long we'd been separated, how often he visited with Bre, and did I know anything about his new girlfriend. The shit was such a turn off. And it irritated me to no end, especially when I was doing my best not to think about Ant and his new wench. When I finally mustered up the courage to tell him that I was over my baby father being the topic of conversation, he tried to spin it as if he just wanted to know what he was getting himself into. I should've been just as concerned with his backstory as he was mine.

His ready-made family smacked me right in the face while we were out to breakfast one day. What was even crazier was when I did meet China, she strolled up with her baby attached to her chest and a mug on her face, but she didn't look the least bit surprised. Kane greeted her and the baby like I was just a coworker he was catching up with. I swear I had to look around for cameras because I just knew I was being pranked. They exchanged a few words, she grilled me hard, and left as quickly as she came. Still, I stuck around, and he basically let me know that China wasn't going anywhere. And for a minute, I found myself going along to get along.

The hand games didn't start until I started to clash with China. The bitch hated my existence, and I wasn't too fond of her ass either. She acted as if I stole her damn man, but as I told her plenty of times, I knew nothing about her prior to meeting her. And as stupid as it may sound, I couldn't shake Kane and made no apologies about it. China and I stayed at each other's throats, and the only way he saw fit to keep us in line was to beat our asses.

One would think that the beatings would make me get the hell on, but in my subconscious mind, Kane wanted me around. I mean, he had everything in China, and she knew him inside and out, yet he still wanted me. The more I found myself falling for Kane, my co-parenting relationship with Ant took a hit. He began to question my decision making, and me being an accomplice in his girlfriend's kidnapping only made me public enemy, alongside Kane. That was completely by force, but Ant wasn't trying to hear that. He took Bre, and I knew for a fact that the only reason why I was still alive now was because of her.

I'd fucked up royally by being in on the plot to snatch Kristen, but the botched kidnapping of her baby had completely blindsided me. There I was, holed up in a hotel for days, in the middle of nowhere after Kane had come by my house in the wee hours of the morning, expressing how much he needed me. His whole demeanor was off, and he had this faraway look in his eyes. I wanted to turn away since he hadn't had the decency to check in on me since we last spoke, but true to my need to be wanted, I caved in. During those couple of days, he didn't talk much, but he clung to me.

I didn't see a spark of energy until yesterday when he stood over me, shaking me from my sleep, demanding that I throw some clothes on. I did as instructed because, although he'd been in a melancholy state, with Kane, it was always best to expect the unexpected. I didn't want any problems. During the drive to our unknown destination, he was quiet, and I opted out of sparking up a conversation. When we pulled into the parking lot of a hospital, I was utterly confused.

"Who's in the hospital?" I finally questioned.

"My baby," he answered with his eyes darting around the parking lot.

"Oh, what happened to Kristine? Is she okay?" I was genuinely concerned and wondered where China was.

"Not Kristine. Kristen just gave birth to our baby. I'm going in to get her. I need you to sit here and keep the car running."

I blinked twice and pulled at my ear to make sure I heard him correctly. There was no way this man was that delusional. "What baby, Kane? And what do you mean you're going in to get her?"

"You're asking too many questions, and right now, I need to think." I looked on as he traded his t-shirt for a white button up and a lab coat from the backseat. Fitted with a pen in the pocket of the lab coat, he checked himself out in the mirror before turning back to me.

"I know you're not going in there to do what I think you're about to do, Kane. And if you are, I won't be here when you come out. Absolutely the fuck not." I shook my head, thinking about him going off the deep end.

"Chloe, getcho Black ass in this driver seat and keep the car running. I'll be back." With that, he got out of the car, and I watched him casually walk into the hospital as if he belonged there.

I sat in the car, gritting my teeth, with my stomach in knots, awaiting his return. Everything in me said to pull off and leave his ass behind, but instead, I waited on pins and needles for what felt like hours. When he finally emerged, I was relieved to see that he was emptyhanded, but by the way he powerwalked to the car, I knew he was steaming inside. Swinging the door open, he got in the passenger seat and slammed it shut.

"Drive!" he barked, making me jump.

Putting the car in drive, I reversed quickly and peeled off. When we returned to the hotel, I made sure to keep quiet and stay out of his way. There was one thing to love someone so much that you couldn't let go, but Kane was psyched out behind Kristen, and that shit sickened me. And now, he wanted me to get my own child involved by making nice with Ant so that I could take her. To Kane, there was no getting what he wanted unless Antwon was dead. No matter what I'd done, I refused to have his blood on my hands.

Watching Kane spiral and turn to getting high confirmed that I needed to put my own plans in motion. After he dropped me back at home, I stayed put for a few days, trying to figure things out. I had to focus on getting back in Ant's good graces so that I could get my baby back and get away from all this shit. I hoped that by me doing so, it would make Kane believe that I was still on his team. I prayed it didn't backfire on me.

SITTING in my car outside Ant's mom's house, I prepared for the worst. It was no secret that Ma Jane couldn't stand the thought of me, but she was one person who agreed that I was a good mother. I just hoped she still felt the same after all that had transpired. With Ant being close to his mother, I was sure that she knew everything. *You're here now, Chloe, might as well pull it in and knock on the door,* I coached myself in my head. I circled the block once more before finding the courage to go up to the door and knock.

As I put my hand up to do so, I stopped and turned back

around. Nope, I wasn't doing this. I wasn't ready to be shut down. I didn't know how I would take being rejected access to my daughter in person. Just as I went to retreat, the door swung open.

"You got a lot of nerve showing up here." Ma Jane's tone held so much aggression that it only made me want to keep walking. "Uhn uhn, you already brought yo' bold ass over here. Come in and face everybody, including yo' child that you basically abandoned." That last part stung, and I wasn't about to be talked down to.

Spinning around, I addressed her. "I've done a lot of things, but I never abandoned my baby. I will not allow you or nobody else to put that on me." I was close to calling her out her name, but I wasn't trying to go there.

"Baby, pick and choose yo' battles wisely cause this ain't what you want. You can miss me with all that extra umph in yo tone, trying to convince me that I'm wrong. I said what the hell I said. Now, you came to my door; you might as well take the extra step." She held the door open wider with her hand on her hip. "Oh, and you betta not have had no unwanted guest trailing you because I'm quick to stand my ground round these parts."

"I'm alone." I assured her, stepping inside.

"Mmmhmm. You walk first cause ion trust you."

As much as it pained me, I kept moving, and the sounds of baby noises and baby talk became more apparent. Entering the room, it felt as if all the air had been sucked out of it. Four pairs of eyes stared directly at me as I stood there like a deer caught in headlights until Bre's voice caught my attention.

"Okay, Kris, I'm done, and I washed my hands too. Can I hold my baby now?" Her little voice did nothing to cut the tension that now filled the room. Kristen didn't answer, her eyes still burning a hole through me, and Ant looked like he wanted to put a bullet in my head. Bre turned her little body in my direction and bolted toward me.

"Mommy!" she shouted with a smile so big it could light up the darkest room. She jumped into my arms, and I wrapped mine around her small frame. My tears soaked the top of her head where her hair was up in a curly puff. I kissed her little cheeks multiple times as she giggled.

"Bre'Ann, go to the room for Daddy. I need to speak to your mom for a minute."

Looking into Ant's eyes as I held onto Bre, his stare held so much hatred. Kristen sat next to him with her baby rested on her shoulder. A part of me wanted to get a good look at the baby to see if it had any features yet. Kane swore up and down the baby was his, and one look would confirm that since he and Ant were two different complexions. I continued to hug Bre tight in fear of her being taken away from me again.

"Come on, Bre. You can help me and Auntie Kaia watch Mani and ya little sister," Maine cut in and stood up with his baby in hand. I was surprised he didn't say anything crazy to me. I didn't miss the hard look though.

"Oh, I'ma go help you get them settled, then I'm coming back out here. I wanna hear what the b-i-t-c-h gotta say." She spelled out the word bitch, I was guessing, because of Bre. Grabbing Kristen's baby from her, she helped escort the kids into the next room, leaving Ant, Kristen, his mom, and me alone.

"Look, I didn't come..." I was cut off before I could finish speaking.

"I don't give a fuck about none of that," Ant gritted, moving toward me. Kristen stopped him before he could fully walk up on me. He turned, and she motioned no with her head. "Nah, fuck that, Kris. She don't get to pick and choose when she wanna be a fucking mother! And she definitely don't get to pop up here knowing she in cahoots with that bitch ass nigga, Kane!" He snatched from her, and I took a step back. Her lip curled, and I was hoping they got into it, leaving me off the hook, but that was wishful thinking.

"Now hold the hell on. Take ya tone down a notch, son. This still my house," his mother warned, pointing a finger in his direction. He grilled her hard, and she matched his intensity. "What, you tryna have a gangsta party up in here? Cause I taught yo' ass that." He backed down. "Now, I ain't feeling this wench either, but she owe everybody an explanation, especially Kristen."

"I didn't come here to start no trouble. I just wanted to see my baby, Antwon. You can't keep me away from her."

"Do you know anything about Kane trying to kidnap my daughter?" Kristen seemed to have found her words.

"No," I answered coldly. Being in her presence made me feel inadequate. She had Ant, Kane was willing to die behind her, and now, she had formed a bond with my daughter.

"Okay," she responded and went to walk off. She didn't get far before she doubled back and charged me. I wasn't quick enough to dodge the barrage of hits she sent my way. "Bitch, you gon' tell me something. Stupid ass hoe!" It went on for a few seconds before she was lifted off me.

"Okay now, boo." Ma Jane spoke to her. "I had to let you get that off, but you're still healing."

"I'm good. I'm good." She shook Ant off her and glared at me. "If I find out you had anything to do with this shit, that ass whipping is going to be the least of your worries. You lucky I love your little girl like my own cause this shit would be so different." Ant shook his head at me and pulled her toward the back.

"You deserved that," Ma Jane said, adding more salt to my open wound. "Now come to this kitchen and get some ice for that eye before Bre come back in here and see you." I stood and followed her to the kitchen. I went to sit down on the barstool, and she stopped me. "No, ma'am. Here's your ice." She handed me an ice pack and folded her arms. "You got a long way to go before you can ever sit at a table of mine."

"And I understand that. I'm not claiming to be an angel, never have. What I need y'all to understand is that little girl in that room belongs to me just as much as she does to Ant. I have rights to her as well. Kristen is not her mother and never will be."

"Your rights didn't mean shit to you when you got caught up with that nigga, Kane," Ant said from behind me. He entered the kitchen and walked around the island to face me. "Understand that you showing up here today don't gain you no fuckin' cool points, Chloe. If it wasn't for Bre's existence, yo' ass would be a permanent memory. And if it wasn't for Kristen, I wouldn't even entertain the thought of letting you see her. Your visits will be supervised until further notice. If you know like I know, you'll stay away from Kane cause he's a dead man walking. Bre, come say bye to yo' mama."

She ran out and gave me a much-needed hug. "What happened to your eye, Mommy?"

"Ummm, I hit it, but I'm okay," I replied, placing the ice pack back on my face. "I love you, and I'll see you soon, so we can go to the park."

"Okay. I love you too."

The last thing I wanted my baby to think was that I was no longer a permanent fixture in her life. I meant what I said when I let them know that Kristen was **not** her mother. And no matter how they felt about me, that would never change. My phone vibrated in my pocket as I left, and when I pulled it out, I sighed, seeing Kane's name flash across the screen.

Now was not the time. I could feel my eye swelling, and my side ached from where I'd fallen to the ground when Kristen snuck me. I ignored the call and rested my head on my steering wheel.

Seeing everybody gathered together, playing family with my daughter, hurt me. Though we'd never been as close, I was still acknowledged as Bre's mother. I was afraid that me falling for the wrong man had fucked up my relationship with my kid, but I was determined to change that. I would go along with the supervised visitation Ant proposed for now but not for long. Bre'Ann Rose Brown was going to be back home with me where she belonged.

CHAPTER 5

Kaia

"You sure we should be doing this right here, right now?" I moaned as Maine assaulted my neck with kisses and pulled at my nipples with his thumb and index finger.

I made the mistake of throwing on a wife beater with no bra when he had the bright idea of coming down to the studio at eleven o'clock at night. Good thing we were over his mother's house spending the night. She wanted to spend time with her grands, and I hated being away from my babies, so I packed a bag for us and them. When we walked in her house, bags in tow, she just shook her head and laughed, calling me a helicopter mom, and that I was. It was rare that you saw me without my two these days.

Maine loved it, but he also enjoyed his quality time to lay up under me when he could or just to get a quickie in here and there. Hence the reason I was in the studio laying down background vocals without the help of an engineer. What was initially supposed to be a first listen for his upcoming album turned into a full make out session. I wasn't sure how we got here, but the way his tongue slid up and down my neck like a snake, I wasn't complaining. I knew he was about to devour the pussy just by the nasty shit he whispered in my ear.

"We good. I locked the door when we first came in. Take that off," he demanded, making my pearl jump at the bass in his tone. I removed my tank top and Nike Pro leggings, leaving my thong on.

Baby girl, I'm coming home. You all mine today, and I'ma hold on tight. I'm on you, and as we lay, we gon' start to play a game. We start to lose track of the time. We don't even care, baby, as we lay.

The lyrics to Casanova's latest single, *Coming Home*, crooned through the state-of-the-art sound system in the studio. Setting my leg up on a nearby chair, Maine pulled my thong to the side and teased my pussy lips with his fingers. I believed he got off on seeing me squirm. Leaning forward, he flattened his tongue and gave my pussy a slow lick, causing my juices to seep out.

"Mmmmm." I bit down on my lip while moaning. Watching him feast on kitty drove me crazy. My body responded to him joyfully. He always took his time indulging in my essence. It was as if he was savoring the moment. He had taken control of my body. Thrusting my hips upward, I was unable to control my orgasm as my sex thumped, and I gave in to the euphoric feeling. "Ughhh, yes, yes, yes."

"Don't tap out on me now, shorty," he taunted me.

I threw my head back as I slowly came down off the high he'd taken me on. Setting my leg down, he sat in the chair and pulled his dick out. It stood straight up in all of its pretty brown glory. Saddling up, I guided him to my sweet spot and gasped as his girth filled me up like it was the first time. My mouth fell open wide, and before I could cry out, he clamped down on my neck again.

"Fuckkk, Tremaine." The dick was so superb I had to call him by his government name. A tear danced down my cheek as he reached spots that even I didn't know existed.

"You hear her, shorty?" I placed my hand over his and guided them to my ass. It didn't take him long to get the hint and spread my cheeks. "Do yo' shit, Ma. Wet this dick up again."

I grinded back and forth on him and squeezed my pussy muscles, heightening the pleasure. I was Meg Thee Stallion with the knees, so it was nothing for me to ride him to a climax. He made sure to fill me up with everything he had too. There was definitely no way I was getting up now.

I laid my bare chest against his, and my head rested in the crook of his neck. "Babe."

"Huh?" he responded lazily. I could feel his heart beating in sync with mine.

"We gotta get up. Didn't you say someone had a session?"

"Yeah, but we good." He kissed my shoulder, and I felt him rise to the occasion again. Smirking, I slid off of him. Seeing my juices on his shaft, my mouth salivated, and I couldn't help wanting to taste myself. "Ughh, shit, Kaia." I took my time taking him down my throat. His hand on my head guiding me up and down let me know I was doing it right. As I got into a groove, loud banging on the studio door made me stop mid suck.

"Shit!" I cursed, hopping up quickly to put my clothes back on. The banging started again, pissing Maine off, who had already put his dick away. I could tell he was now stalling so that I could get dressed. "I'm good now, babe. You can open the door." Reaching for my phone, I dialed Ma Jane's number to check on the kids. It was getting real late now, and I had only heard one song from the album as we were more focused on making music of our own.

"Hey, I didn't think you'd be here this late. Oh, hey, Kaia." Seeing Simone enter the studio, my mood shifted, but I made sure that my body language didn't show it.

She was chipper in her greeting to Maine, but you could hear the enthusiasm die down when she addressed me. The bitch could miss me with the dry hi. I wasn't beat for the fake shit. We had already drawn a line in the sand. I got comfortable in the chair and went to playing a game of Solitaire on my phone.

"Yeah. I wanted my baby to get a first listen of the album before it releases next week," Maine said, clearly trying to recover from the cold shoulder I threw.

"Ahh, man. Girl, you are so lucky. I've been practically begging this guy to let me listen to the album." She playfully punched his arm. Only I didn't see it as playful but open flirting. "Being all secretive and shit. Now that you're done with your album, you can come and bless me on mine."

There was that twinkle again. Did she not know that I was working on me? I was someone's mother now, so I was learning to choose my battles wisely. This heffa was acting like she wanted war. I gave Maine a look, and with him being so in tune with me, he read my mind. Sitting next to me, he kissed my cheek and threw my legs across his.

"You here to do some recording?" She'd been so focused on Maine's attachment to me that her response was delayed.

"Oh, umm, yeah. Playboy should be here in a minute. We're gonna lay down some tracks. I've been in high demand after our performance." I went to stand, and Maine's hand gripped my thigh.

"Tread lightly, babes, tread lightly," I warned. She was begging for me to go across her shit. The air got real thick with Maine still rubbing my thigh. Simone tried to avert her eyes from mine and went to doing something with the soundboard. Playboy entering the studio was a great distraction.

"Yurrr," he called out in a jovial tone. Anytime Playboy was around, he was upbeat. "Damn, who died?" I couldn't help but snicker. I loved when he was around. He always had jokes.

"Nobody. You ready?" Simone snapped.

"Slow down, gangsta. I just got here. Let me greet my people," he said before bopping in our direction. Maine gave him a brotherly hug, and he went to kiss my cheek.

"Nigga, I'll beat yo' ass," Maine threatened while pushing Playboy away from me. We both laughed.

"My bad, my bad. Sis, had I known you were here, I would've brought Sha loudmouth ass. She called me all types of motherfuckas for coming out this late. Oh, and she said when she see you, she gon' give you a piece of her mind, songstress." He looked in the direction of Simone, and her eyebrows curled up. "She just playing though." He tried to make light of the threat.

I knew my girl, and there was nothing playful about it. Sha meant exactly what she said, and I didn't blame her. Simone was one slick bitch, but I was slicker. Shanice and Play had been going strong since the day she introduced Mecca and I to him at the studio a while ago. That was the first day I actually enjoyed being around Maine.

"I'm ready to get back to Ma's house." I let Maine know.

Standing up, I walked toward the door with him trailing behind me.

"Give him a hit, Simone," Maine coached. I went to say something but thought better of it. In the car, he had one hand on my thigh while the other gripped the steering wheel.

"I'm really proud of you, baby. Although I didn't get to hear the full album, the one song I did hear I loved." He put my hand to his mouth and kissed the back of it.

"Thank you, shorty. And thank you for keeping yo' cool back there with Simone." I only nodded my head in response. "How you feel about me doing a joint album with her?" I didn't answer immediately, and I could feel his eyes on the side of my head. I was the last person to ask such a question.

"I think whatever is best for the company is what you should do."

"Come on. Don't do that. Tell me how you really feel."

"You already know how I feel about her, and it's clear that she is very fond of you. Heavy on the fond part too. I think the album would be a hit though. There's no doubting her talent." I wasn't thrilled about the idea, but I was his biggest fan. This was Maine's dream, and I wasn't going to stand in the way of him living it. I had to get with the program. My job was to be his support system, and that I would do.

"Shorty, the last thing I want is for you to harbor any ill

feelings about the way I move. Your trust in me is everything. I can assure you that ain't shit going on other than music."

"I trust you, bae."

"Aight."

We made it back to Ma Jane's, checked on the kids, and settled ourselves in the guest bedroom. It didn't take long after I rested my head on the pillow before I was counting sheep. I couldn't have been sleep long before I felt Maine slip out of the bed. Peeking up at the clock, it read a quarter to four. I watched in the darkness as he redressed himself and made sure to shut my eyes when he leaned over the bed. Placing a kiss on my cheek, he whispered he loved me and left the room. And this was the part where Tremaine Brown had me fucked up.

Simone

As it rained down on my head, mud and dirt surrounded my feet. All I could think was, how did I get here? I wanted nothing more than to knock Kane over the head with the shovel I used to help him dig a big enough hole to put China in. I was officially an accomplice to murder — all in the name of wanting to uphold my image as this big R&B superstar who had it all together. But the truth was, my life was in shambles. And so long as I had an attachment to Kane, I was attached to chaos.

"You have to dig faster, Simone. This rain is coming down, and soon, this flashlight will be of no use to us." Kane's voice made me cringe. I had come to the realization that the urgency and emotion *he expressed when he first called me was a whole fucking act. He was unhinged.*

"I'm digging as fast as I can. I can't see shit, Kane!" I snapped at him. Glancing up at the black plastic bag that held China's body, I hung my head. From my understanding, she had been in love with Kane for as long as forever. They were best friends turned lovers, so it seemed so surreal to be burying her body in the makeshift grave.

It was another hour before we were done, and I smelled just as bad as I felt. Throwing the shovel in the trunk of his car, I made sure to slam the door once I was in the passenger seat. I wanted him to know that I had a fucking attitude. Not only was I caught up in this whole operation get Kristen bullshit, but I now had a one-way ticket to hell behind this bastard.

Dropping me off at my apartment, he left me with a parting reminder. "Don't go growing a conscious and feeling like you need to clear that shit. Remember, no matter how famous you are, I still have the power to destroy you."

I regretted the day I turned to him for help. He only reminded me of why I fought hard to stay away from my family all these years. Kane felt like he owned me because of the tape he had. Had I known that being an accomplice to murder would be how I'd be repaying my debt, I would've put the tape out myself for the world to see my whole ass. Right now, he had me by the throat, and he knew it.

My days had been such a blur since the night we buried China. I hadn't been to the studio until tonight and seeing

Maine hugged up with Kaia put a sour taste in my mouth. My mission per Kane was to now get close to Maine. Somewhere along the way, my heart got involved, and I became smitten with the man. That was a big mistake on my part. I did my best to keep my feelings at bay at first, but when he opened the door for friendship, I walked right through it with a smile.

He was easy to talk to and didn't judge me. Although I hated when he was brash at times, I was turned on by it. Me falling for his unorthodox charm was what had Kane breathing down my neck for results. I could've pissed on myself when he showed up to the lunch I had with Kaia. I thanked my lucky stars that he'd just missed her by a few seconds. Seeing Maine tonight only reaffirmed why I couldn't be on board with anything that had to do with harming him.

I felt something for him. I was unsure whether it was love or infatuation, but it was something. He saw past the star I was right now. He saw the star I was becoming. I was willing to go to war over that feeling, even if it was against my own flesh and blood or his woman.

"Yo, songstress, we making a hit or you gonna sit in the booth with the long face? And if so, let me call my lady and let her know it's gonna be a long night." Playboy spoke through the intercom. He always had a joke readily available whether it was the right time or not.

"I'm ready. I wrote something last night. It was to the

melody of that Teairra Mari song, *Phone Booth*. Can you do something with the beat, like make it your own?"

"Don't insult me, songstress. You know this is what I do. Gimmie a minute and issa hit."

I pulled out my phone to go over the lyrics I jotted down during another sleepless night. As I went to unlock it, a text message popped up on the screen. Seeing that it was Kane, I sighed and navigated to our text thread.

Rain: I haven't heard from you. You know what happens when I don't hear from you, Simone.

Me: I've been busy. I'm in the studio right now. I'll call you as soon as I can.

Rain: You haven't been talking, have you?

Me: There's nothing to talk about. Call you when I can.

I deleted the text thread where I had Kane saved under the name Rain. I wanted to be extra careful in case my phone ever went missing.

"I'm ready, Play." I motioned to him with a head nod and readjusted the Beats headphones on my head.

As soon as the beat purred through the expensive headphones, I sang the song from the depths of my soul. Playboy had brought the acoustics in enough for the song to be a ballad. I sang a song of an unexpected love and wanting a thug to treat me right. The lyrics described a longing so fierce that it kept you up all night craving for that person. I belted them out and held a high note at the end. It was so smooth I knew there wouldn't be a need for another take.

"How was that?" I asked, removing the headphones and taking a sip of my tea with lemon.

"Come out real quick." I frowned at his tone and went to join him at the soundboard.

"Wassup, you didn't like it?" My lip hung in disappointment. I had put my all into the song.

"Keep it a stack. You in love with my boy?" There wasn't a smirk on his face nor a hint of laughter in his tone. How the hell did he get that from a song? Damn, was I that obvious?

"What?" I looked at him, feigning ignorance. "Stop playing with me, Play. Do you like the song or not?" I was getting agitated because he had put me out there. Although it was just me and him in the studio, all of a sudden, I felt exposed.

"I guess that's a yes. Damn, I had a feeling, but I didn't want it to be true. Shit, I owe Sha a stack now," he cursed himself.

"I don't know what you're talking about." I denied again, keeping my face as straight as possible.

"That's right, deny deny. Don't ever tell nobody the truth. Kaia is nothing to be played with, especially when it comes to Maine and vice versa." I turned my lip up at the mention of Kaia's name. "The lyrics are dope as hell though. I got a little Jazmine Sullivan soul vibe while you were in there. This for the album?"

"Yeah, I want it to be my first single." I perked up again.

"Aight, I'm sure Ant wouldn't have a problem with that.

Let me do some mixing and we can get up outta here." We stayed and recorded for another couple of hours and ended up leaving the studio at almost five in the morning.

"You sure you don't need me to follow you home? My girl already gon' have my head, so it's the least I can do," Play offered while punching in the numbers on his phone to activate the alarm for the building.

"I'm a big girl. I'm perfectly capable of driving my own car home. Goodnight, Play, and thank you for coming out to record for me." He nodded and waited until I was in my car before he drove off. Securing myself in my seat belt, I put my car in reverse. As I went to pull out of the parking spot, I felt a presence behind me.

Turning around quickly, I saw nothing in my backseat and did my best to shake the eerie feeling I had whenever I was alone. It had been happening ever since I aided Kane in burying China. I didn't get out of my parking spot good before my phone rang in my bag. Reaching over to the passenger side, I went to pick it up when I felt the car moving backward on its own.

"Oh, shit," I yelled out, dropping my phone in a panic as I stepped on the brake, quickly shifting the car in park. I was scared shitless when I saw the headlights of a car through my rearview mirror. I quickly hit the locks on my car, scared to get out. Who the hell would be out at this time of night and even worse, pulling in behind me? Snatching up my phone again, I went to dial Play to see how far he'd gone. A sudden knock at my door made me jump, but I refused to look out the window.

"So, you just gon' tap my bumper then act like you don't see me at this window?" Maine's voice surprised me, and a smile graced my face as I turned to face him. He motioned for me to roll down the window. "Everything alright?"

"Yeah, sorry about that. My foot must've hit the gas while I was reaching for my phone. Shit, did I really hit your car?" I went to open the door, so I could see for myself. He stepped back, allowing me to assess the damage.

"It's not that bad, just a little scratch."

"I am so sorry. I'll pay for the damage. One second, let me grab my purse." I scurried back to my car, feeling like a real dummy. "What are you doing back here?" I questioned, opening my purse to get my checkbook.

"I left my phone inside. Hey," he put his hand over mine, and my heart leaped, "you good. Don't worry about no money. It's just a scratch."

"Yeah, just a scratch on a Bentley truck. You crazy as hell if you think I'm not paying you for it." He laughed, and it sounded like music to my ears. I was making him laugh. I relished in the moment.

"If it makes you feel any better, it's a month old." I joined in on the laughter. "Since I don't want you running into anything else, let me go in here and get my phone then move my truck."

I gave him a nod, and he walked off. Just a few minutes

ago, I was rushing to pull off because of the eerie feeling, but knowing Maine was nearby, I felt better. It didn't take long for him to return, and I went to hop back in my car.

"Thanks," I said, wrapping my arms around his neck for a quick hug. His cologne tickled my nose, and all I could think about was him bending me over the hood and fucking me senseless. He gave me a friendly pat on the back, and I reluctantly released him.

"Aight, send a text to the company group chat when you get home so we know you made it in safely."

He was concerned. That said a lot. I would be sure to send that text, along with an attachment, just not to the group chat. I didn't need to be a part of Kane's plan to lure Maine in. I wanted him to myself, and I was willing to lay it all on the line for him.

Maine

The next morning, I woke up to Kaia sitting on top of me. It was not in the inviting way I would have liked either. Her face was screwed up, her arms were crossed tightly on her chest, and she had a blank stare. She wasn't the least bit moved by the morning wood that I was sure she felt rubbing against the seat of her panties.

"Wassup, shorty?" I finally spoke through a yawn after we had a stare off that lasted a few seconds.

"Where'd you go last night?"

"Back to the studio. I left my phone. Lift up." I tapped her thigh, but she didn't budge. "I gotta piss, Kaia. Lift up, bae."

She kept her eyes on me as she lifted her body from

mine, giving me room to get up. Stretching, I stood from the bed to head to the bathroom, and she was right on my heels.

"Okay, bumped into Simone?" She asked a question it was clear she already knew the answer to, so I didn't bother responding. She watched me like a hawk while I took a piss. Giving my dick two quick shakes, I tucked it away and went to wash my hands and brush my teeth. "I see you playing this morning. Cool, I hope yo' ass choke."

She went to walk out, and I grabbed her by her waist, pulling her back to me. "Why you wanna beef with me early in the morning, shorty? And yes, I did see Simone. In fact, she bumped into my truck as she was pulling out of the parking lot. Wassup, why you acting so hostile? You supposed to love on yo' man from the time I open my eyes in the morning til' the time I close them at night."

"Check yo' phone and let me know if I have a reason to be hostile." Pushing me off her, she left the bathroom.

If she was insisting on me checking my phone, I already knew whatever was in there wasn't anything good. I shook my head, following behind her. While she left the room, I went straight for the phone. Picking it up, there were no notifications on the screen. I then pulled down the notification bar and knew just why Kaia was in her feelings. "What the fuck is wrong with this girl?" I said out loud as I read Simone's message.

Simone B: I made it home safely. Thank you for everything (kissy face emoji).

I specifically told her to hit the company group chat for this very reason. This slick shit she pulled would make me look suspect no matter what I said to Kaia.

"I can tell by that stuck look on your face that you read the text," Kaia said, reentering the room with Mani attached to her breast and a cover up wrapped around her. She had taken to motherhood so quickly that you would've thought she'd done it before. Everything was about the well-being of Kymani and Chase; for that, I admired my lady even more.

"I'll check the emoji shit. That was out of line. I did tell her to text when she got home, but the company group chat, not me. And I only told her that cause it was late, and it was the nice thing to do, right?"

"If you looking for confirmation, then I don't know what to tell you. But you better tell her to stop playing with me though. That hoe ain't dumb, and she knows what she's doing. The fact that you keep entertaining it behooves me."

"What am I entertaining, Kaia? Would you rather me not talk to the girl? We on the same label, and I socialize with her on the same level I do everybody else."

"Tremaine, since when yo' ass become a fuckin' socialite? Like be for real. Let me make it plain to you. That bitch want you, and she will openly flirt and do little slick shit like that text to get next to you. What I'm not gonna do is keep mentioning it because you round here actin' real clueless, and that's losing me. I hope what I'm saying isn't going in one ear and out the other."

"I don't see no other woman but you, shorty."

"I love you, Tremaine, but I know a problem when I see one. If you don't address it, it'll get worse." She left the room, and I sighed. Deleting the message Simone sent, I texted my brother.

Bro: *Need to chop it up with you.*

He texted back for me to meet him at his house, and I got ready to do that.

"Hey, son, what's going on?" My mom spoke, not tearing her eyes from the TV, when I walked in. Just to fuck with her, I stood in front of it. "Boy, if you don't move. Yo' daddy for damn sure wasn't no glass maker." I laughed and sat down on the couch beside her. "What you do to Kaia?"

"How you know Kaia ain't do nothing to me?" I countered.

"You right, so what happened?"

"How you know something happened?"

She looked over at me, and I smirked. "Tremaine, you want me to cuss yo' ass out?"

"She mad at the way I interact with one of my label mates. I left out last night because I left my phone at the studio, and the girl just happened to be there."

"This the Simone girl, right?" I stared at the side of her face, wondering what all she knew. "Sometimes just your mere presence can spark a flame in someone that burns long after you're gone. It takes that one interaction for a woman to feel that you're the one."

Tapping my arm, she got up and left me sitting on the couch, confused as fuck. *Simone thinks I'm the one?*

"READ BETWEEN THE LINES, BRO." Play motioned with his hands, and Ant couldn't stop laughing. We were over Ant's crib, chilling in his basement, the area where we did man shit only.

"What's wrong with this nigga, bro?" I pointed to Play but directed my question to my brother. I had just finished telling them about my run in with Simone, and it seemed like Play knew something I didn't.

"She want you, dawg. I mean, like want you want you. She has the potential to fuck up ya home."

"Only if he let it happen," Ant added. "And we ain't even built like that."

"Facts. I don't even know why you put that shit in the atmosphere, Play. I already got Kaia on my head about it. Simone starting to cause me problems with the silly shit. Problems that I don't need. I would hate to become the nigga that y'all know I can be, but I ain't about to keep having static at the crib because of a broad havin' a crush on a nigga."

"Yo, we got more alarming shit to tend to. Like the fact that this hoe ass nigga, Kane, still breathing the same air as us. It's not sittin' well with me, ain't been sittin' well with me. I need to understand how this nigga is managing to pop up where we are without any one of us knowing. This pussy tried to kidnap my baby girl, dawg." Ant exhaled his frustrations.

"You ain't get nothing outta Chloe?" I was still blown at the fact that he was allowing her to be around Bre, even if it was supervised. Yeah, she was her mom, but she had already shown disloyalty. Kris was the perfect mother figure for Bre. I kept my thoughts to myself unless I was asked though.

"She tight lipped as shit. She gave me a number for him, but the number was disconnected. What she don't know is I have Malcolm tracking her calls. So far, no calls in or out from Kane."

"You a better man than me, fam," Play expressed, and I had to dap him up.

"That's the thing. Kristen is the reason for this new arrangement," he scoffed. "She keep with this whole Chloe is Bre's mom bullshit."

That shit still didn't make sense to me. Chloe was an opp and would remain that as far as I was concerned. I never understood what Ant saw in her anyway. "Aight, look, we need to get back to the essence of what it is that we were doing before this music shit popped off."

"Back on our bully?" Play questioned for confirmation.

"I don't know any other way around it at this point. All this tryna draw a nigga out and being strategic because of the image in this music shit has gotten us nowhere. That nigga, Kane, may be in hiding, but wherever he is, he's getting a laugh at our expense, and I ain't gon' keep being on the losing end." Mecca came to mind, and I shook my head. The loss was still fresh. "I'ma link with Dino and put something in motion."

"I'm meeting with Ross later on too. If he don't tell me what I wanna hear, I'm putting his ass on desk duty." What was understood didn't need to be explained.

We talked more and were interrupted by my ringing phone. Seeing an incoming call from an unknown number, I walked out of the room to answer it.

"**Hello.**" A stern voice spoke on the other end.

"**Who dis?**" I replied just as sternly.

"**This is Detective Pierce from the thirteenth precinct. Am I speaking with Tremaine Brown?**"

"**Speaking.**"

"**I'm calling regarding Ms. Kandice Thompson. Would you mind coming down to the station to answer some questions for me?**"

"**What questions do you need to ask at the station that you can't ask over the phone?**" Whoever this clown was, he didn't know I was a vet at this shit. It had been a couple months since I rid myself of my Kandice problem. And like any other plays I made, I was discreet and meticulous about it.

"**Sir, as you know, this is a sensitive matter. I believe it's best to have this conversation in person. I would like to think that you'd want your son's mother found as soon as**

possible." He was trying to bait me, and unfortunately for him, I knew how to detach myself from my emotions.

"I never knew she was missing. I'll tell you what, Detective Pierce. Let me move some things around and I'll be right down." I disconnected the call before he could respond.

"Bro, you straight?" Ant asked from the doorway.

"I gotta make a run real quick. I'ma hit you when I'm in the clear."

"Whoa, what the hell going on?"

"Kandice," was all I said before taking the steps two at a time until I made it upstairs. Ant already knew what that meant, so we didn't have to speak the obvious. The only people who knew what really happened to Kandice was us. I was sure Kaia had her own ideas, although she never voiced them.

"Aye, shorty," I called out to Kaia from where she was seated in the living room with Shanice, Kristen, and the kids. My solo trip had quickly turned to a family trip to Ant's. Chase lay in her lap, asleep, while Mani and Kenzie lay in a playpen. I had to laugh at the two of them looking like they were having their own conversation. Chase hadn't missed out on any love because both Kaia and I gave him that plus more. Kaia spoiled him so bad. I couldn't tell her nothing about her *handsome man.* "I need to holla at you real quick." I motioned with my head for her to come to me. She got up, and I ushered her into the kitchen for privacy.

"Wassup, why you look so serious?"

"I gotta go down to the precinct real quick. They wanna ask me some questions about Kandice." Her facial expression went blank, and I grabbed her hand. "Chill out, don't start overthinking. I'm good. I just wanted to put you on."

"If you good, I'm going with you. I'm sure Sha wouldn't mind holding the kids down." She went to walk away, and my voice halted her steps.

"Nah, I need you to be here with the kids. You gotta trust me, Kaia."

"I do trust you."

"Then trust that I got us. I'll be back. I promise." I kissed her forehead and went to do the same to the kids and headed to my car. I didn't get to shift the gear before the passenger side door flew open. I looked at Kaia as she hopped her little ass in my truck.

"Come on and drive so we can get this over with." Her little feisty ass didn't listen for shit.

IT DIDN'T TAKE LONG to get downtown. When we pulled up, she went to get out, and I stopped her. "Sit yo' little ass down. You not going inside. I'll be right back."

"Maine, I..."

"No, Kaia. I've been letting you do too much as it is. Don't make me get on that typa time witchu, shorty. You pushing it for real. I understand you wanna be there for me, and I appreciate and love you for it, but when I say something, take heed. This shit is not up for debate. Now, keep the car running, yo eyes open, and sit still."

Sighing, she conceded. "Okay."

"Aight." Pressing my lips against hers, I squeezed her thigh and got out the car.

I swaggered into the precinct with my hat covering my eyes. Unlike being known for slanging bricks, people were in my face constantly for an autograph or picture since the music had taken off. I was still getting used to the limelight, so half the time, I didn't have security with me.

"I'm here to see Detective Pierce." I told the big breasted lady at the desk.

"Name," she responded with a nasty attitude.

I could've bombed on her mean ass, but I gave her a pass. "Brown." I gave her my last name.

"Wait, you're Maine, like Maine the rapper." Her voice squeaked, and she clapped her hands like it was a celebration. "Oh, my God, I love ya music so much. *The One* is my shit. Ooh, can I get yo' autograph?"

"Right now is not the time, Ma. Can you go get the detective for me?"

"Oh, damn, you can't sign an autograph for a fan? You one of those celebrities, huh? Let me get Detective Pierce for you. I can't wait to tell my homegirl about this." She walked off, and I was happy she did because I was about to cuss her big, manly looking ass out.

"Thank you for coming, Mr. Brown," the detective held the door to the interrogation room open for me.

"How can I help you?" I opted out of sitting; I didn't plan on staying long.

"Well, as I stated over the phone, Ms. Thompson has been reported missing. Her mother came down to the station a couple days ago to make the report. According to her, you and Ms. Thompson share a child and hadn't been getting along lately. When's the last time you spoke to her?" He pulled out a pad to start writing down what I said.

"I could've saved myself the trip and told you over the phone that the last time I spoke to Kandice was in regard to getting my son. And she and I got along well enough to co-parent." I maintained a straight face that he couldn't read.

"Where's your son now?"

"With family."

"Well, I'm going to be honest with you. Ms. Thompson's mother believes you have something to do with her disappearance. What's your take on that?"

"My take is that I wouldn't benefit from Kandice being missing. Now, if you excuse me, I have business that I need to attend to. If there's any other questions you may have, feel free to direct them to my lawyer, Jeffrey Klein." Turning, I made my way to the door. "Oh, and while her mother has me on the top of her suspect list, ask her why she hasn't reached out in regards to her grandson's well-being." I walked out of the precinct and right into a barrage of reporters.

"Maine, why are you coming out of the precinct?"

"Does this have anything to do with your past as a drug dealer?"

I pushed through the reporters and made it back to my truck without incident.

"What the hell was that all about?" Kaia asked with a worried expression. I ignored her and dialed Ant on speaker-phone, pulling out from in front of the precinct.

"Bro, tell me something."

"We got another problem on our hands."

Kristen

I stopped reaching out to China altogether when my text messages went unanswered after a couple days. I hadn't spoken it into the universe, but I was starting to feel like something bad had happened to her. If that was the case, I was sure that Kane was connected to her bad luck in some way. I decided to leave the situation alone and let Ant handle it. Besides, I'd taken on new responsibilities.

I didn't know where I found it in me to be the bigger person when it came to dealing with Chloe, but I did. Motherhood had given me a whole new outlook on things. Though she had played a hand in my kidnapping, she didn't participate in the abuse. She basically chose to turn a blind eye and not speak up. For that, we'd never be cool, and she knew to tread lightly with me after what happened at Ma Jane's house. At the end of the day, I didn't want Bre to have to miss out on time with her mother because of an adult situation. That said, I had to keep my ill feelings in check and conduct myself accordingly.

Ant didn't share my reasoning at all, which was why he chose not to deal with Chloe. He left it up to me to make the planned weekend visits. We always met in a public place, and Ant made sure I had security with me at all times. I also carried my own protection around. I was being the bigger person, not the biggest dummy. I didn't trust Chloe either. During the outings, we didn't speak unless Bre was engaged in the conversation. Today was our third meet up. We were going to the movies.

"It's not awkward being around her after what happened?" Sha questioned as we chopped it up in my living room.

I shrugged my shoulders. "It's not the best feeling in the world, but I have to keep in the back of my mind that I'm doing this for Bre, ya know? She loves her mom, and she's at the age where she's asking questions, and I don't want to be the reason why Ant can't answer them."

"I get what you're saying. I swear you have to be one of the strongest people I know. Had it been me, I'd bat that bitch upside her head every time I saw her face. Like What happened?" She threw her hands like she was prepared to fight, and I was rolling. Being around her made me feel like Mecca was still here.

"Girl, don't think I don't have those feelings at times. Maybe I should trip her when we leaving out the theatre. You know, since it'll be dark, she won't think it's on purpose. It'll be a reminder that a bitch ain't forget what happened."

"Hello! Now that's what I'm talkin' bout. We can't be round here making a bitch think shit sweet." Laughing, we slapped fives.

"Aight, I'm ready to go. I'm high and horny," Play announced, entering the living room.

"Well, you better get alert and goofy because we're on baby duty. Kaia left with Maine." I chuckled at the look of disappointment etched in his face. "You might as well pick up ya lip cause wasn't nothing happening anyway, Mr. I Need to Make This Late-Night Studio Run."

"Don't do my boy like that, Sha," Ant cosigned and dapped Play. "He's a hot producer right now. He gon' have to keep up that momentum, sis. Late nights are a part of the deal."

"Late nights while you're already out is different than getting out the bed at almost midnight to go record a song. I'm sorry. That's just not gonna work for me. Especially when it's with Simone hot pussy ass." I slapped fives with her again, agreeing one hundred and ten percent.

"Okay, alright with all that slapping hands shit. I ain't wanna hang with you no way. I'ma chill with my god kids.

Help me pack them up." He grabbed Chase and his things while Shanice grabbed Kymani, and they left out.

"Where's Bre?" I asked Ant.

"Upstairs getting dressed. Did I tell you how much I hate this arrangement you have going on with her egg donor?" I rolled my eyes at him and went to pick Kenzie up from her playpen to get her dressed. I already knew how he felt and didn't need a constant reminder.

"You never forget to express that to me, babe. You seem to forget that I was the one she fucked over. Let's just keep focus on the big picture. Like you tell me, everything isn't always about you." Knowing the conversation could lead to a potential argument, I busied myself with Kenzie. He sat across from me, burning a hole through my forehead. I knew he wanted to press the issue. I was happy to hear Bre's little footsteps as she came downstairs.

"I'm ready, Kris," she announced. She was cute in her brown corduroy skirt overalls with a white cheetah print shirt underneath it. Her chestnut brown Uggs paired well with the outfit. "Daddy, where my scarf thingy like Kris'?" she asked, referring to the infinity scarf I bought her to match mine.

"Should be in your room. I didn't wear it." She giggled before running off to her room to find it.

"Found it." She came back with the scarf wrapped around her neck and her coat on.

"Okay, boo, we gonna drop sissy off first, and then we're off to the movies to meet with your mommy."

"Yay, I can't wait to see *The Lion King* again." This would be our fourth trip to the movies to see the same movie. I was bound to fall asleep. Ant walked us out to the car, and after whispering something to my security detail, he made his way to us.

"Smile, give your face a break, baby," I teased and kissed his lips. He locked both Kenzie and Bre in their car seats and told me he loved us. Leaning into me, he recited his same statement he made whenever it was time to meet up with Chloe.

"Watch that bitch, Kristen. If something seems off, it's off. A snake gon' always be a snake." I took heed to his words every time.

We were running late, but I figured as long as we made it, that was all that mattered. Pulling up to the AMC theatres on 42nd Street, I knew for sure we wouldn't find parking. I instructed our security to find a parking garage and come into the theatre when he was done. I had already purchased tickets online, so we wouldn't have to wait. I really wanted to go to IPIC theatre in Jersey, but Chloe chose here. I hated 42nd Street. It was always crowded with tourists and quite overrated. However, I put my feelings on the back burner and went with it.

"Ooh, there go Mommy right there," Bre yelled in excitement, trying to break free of me and run toward Chloe, who stood by the ticket machines.

"Uhn uhn, Bre'Ann. You can't run off like that, boo. You see all these people in here? You hold my hand until we get to her, okay?" She nodded, and once we got closer, I let her hand go for her to go sprinting.

"Hey, my favorite girl in the whole wide world," Chloe boasted, swopping Bre up in her arms. "Thank you for bringing her, Kristen." I gave a simple smile. She placed Bre back on her feet, and instinctively, we both went for her hand. I went to move mine to let her have the moment.

"You can hold my hand too, Kris." Bre assured me, making me smile at how thoughtful she was. I caught the frown on Chloe's face before she turned it to a phony smile.

Once in the theatre, I got comfortable in my seat while Bre sat in the middle of us with a big tub of popcorn in front of her. There was no chance in hell I was watching *The Lion King* again. I discreetly held Bre's hand so that if she made any sudden movements, I'd feel it and wake up. I woke up a little while later to applause and Chloe and Bre standing up. The movie was over, and the nap had me feeling energized.

"I gotta pee," Bre said, doing the pee pee dance.

"Me too," Chloe added. "Come on, Bre Bre. I'll take you."

I went to say no but wanted to give her the benefit of the

doubt. So, instead, I followed close behind them until they made it to the bathroom. Not wanting to stand at the door, I stood off to the side and Facetimed my mom. She was watching Kenzie for me.

"Where my baby?" I said once the call connected. I smirked, knowing my mother was going to chew me out about my greeting.

"Excuse me, let me hang up so you can go find the sense that I gave you." I laughed at her facial expression.

"My bad, Mommy. Hey, where my baby? Can you put her on the phone, so she can see me?"

"You act like this child can talk," she fussed, turning the camera around. I smiled at her lying next to her gpa. I was sure he had her watching some kind of sports.

"My baby don't like ESPN, Dad. She likes *Mickey Mouse Clubhouse*," I teased.

"She like whatever I like while she here. Now go find you some business. We over here bonding." He waved me off like I was standing in front of him.

"Where's Bre?" my mother asked, putting the camera back on herself.

"Bathroom with Chloe. They've been in there a little minute. Let me go check on them." I walked over to the bathroom to see what was taking so long seeing as there wasn't a line for the stalls. "Bre... Chloe," I called out amongst the couple of ladies that were in the bathroom. With no immediate response from Bre, I started to panic. My mouth became extremely dry as I tried to swallow. "Ma... they not here."

She sat up quickly, and the phone looked like it was almost pressing against her face. "Kristen," she spoke in a calm voice, "ask one of the people in the bathroom if they seen them, baby."

"Excuse me." I tapped a lady who was fixing her makeup at the sink. "Did you see a little girl with a brown corduroy overall skirt and a brown coat? She had a curly ponytail and would've been with a lady in a red peacoat."

"Yeah, they walked out the other side a minute ago." My heart sank. How could I forget that this theatre had two entrances for the bathroom?

"Thank you." I rushed back out. "Ma, I gotta call you back." I hung up and shoved my phone in my coat pocket. I ran straight for the exit, shouting Bre's name. "Bre'Ann... Bre!" I screamed like a mad woman on the busy streets of Times Square. Neither Bre nor Chloe were anywhere in sight. Pulling out my phone again, I smashed my fingers on the dial pad, dialing Chloe's number.

"Come on, you selfish, grimy ass bitch, pick up," I said aloud as the phone rang and rang, only for no one to pick up. I tried again, and it went straight to voicemail. Fuck! I had been taken for a fool and let Chloe kidnap her own fucking child.

CHAPTER 9

Ant

If it's not one thing it's another, I thought to myself as I sat in my car outside of Ross' house, waiting for him to come out. Hearing from Maine that Kandice's mother was trying to make him a suspect in her disappearance was a fire I wasn't prepared to put out. No sooner than I hung up the phone with him, our publicist called.

"Care to tell me why I received a call about Maine walking out of the precinct not too long ago?"

"It's a family matter."

"A family matter that has the potential to affect your business if we don't get ahead of it and soon."

"And that's what I pay you for, to get ahead of it. Right

now, I need to deal with this personal matter in house, and when the time comes to address the public, I'll be sure to tag you in."

"You do that. We have a big tour coming up, and it's a lot of money on the line. We can't afford any distractions." She spoke as if I didn't know what was on the line. Hell, it was me that was financing it.

"Need I remind you that it's my money we're talkin' about? I'll keep you posted, Shardae."

Hanging up with her, I sent Ross a text, telling him to hurry the fuck up. A minute later, he came out in his uniform with a bag over his shoulder. He looked both ways before getting in on the passenger side. The door closed, and I pulled off. No words were exchanged until we got to our destination, which was the diner we used to meet up at when it was time for me to pay him.

"If you're hitting me up to see me and I'm no longer on payroll, I know this can't be good," he said after waving the waitress over to take our order.

"You already know why I'm here. You knew from the moment I texted ya phone."

"What can I get you guys?" the waitress asked just before he could respond.

"Coffee with cream and sugar and a warm croissant for me."

"And for you?" She batted her eyes.

"Nothing," I stated flatly. Clearly not caring for my tone, she walked off with an attitude.

"He came to see me a couple weeks back, wanting me to get on board with some operation take you down type shit. As you can see, I turned it down." I sat back, analyzing his body language. His eyes said he was being truthful. "He's really obsessed with that Kristen chick, man. He even thinks her baby is his."

Banging on the table, I leaned over it. "That nigga ain't no kin to my fuckin' kid," I spat through gritted teeth. I swore I'd never wanted to murk somebody so bad that I could taste it. "Gimmie an address."

"Wish I could. Right now, I don't know where he is." I thanked Ross for what little he gave me and decided not to press any further. "If it means anything, I didn't have nothing to do with this shit he pulled. You and your brother have always been good to me."

"I know you didn't. Trust me, you would've been dead soon as you walked out your front door. The uniform means little to nothing to me. Catch an Uber. I got somewhere to be." I threw a twenty on the table and headed back out. My phone vibrated in my hand with an incoming call from Kris as soon as I reached my car.

"Wassup, babe, everything good?" I could hear her sniffling, and that told me that shit wasn't good at all.

"No." She sniffled. **"Everything is not good, Antwon. She**

took Bre. I turned my back for two fucking minutes, and she took her. Baby, I'm sooo sorry. I should've listened to you." She was now breaking down, and I couldn't stop the tears that fell from my eyes. "Antwon, baby, please answer me."

"I'm here, Ma. We gon' find her. This shit not your fault." My mouth said that, but I really didn't know how I felt. My body had gone numb. I had to get my baby girl back, and I was putting a bullet between Chloe's eyes. "Where you at?"

"Sitting in front of Chloe's apartment. I swear to God, if I see her walking in this building, I'ma rag this stupid bitch!"

"Stay right there. Don't move!" The fact that she knew where Chloe lived was the least of my worries. I needed answers. I did eighty on the highway to her place. The only thing that gave me solace was the fact that I knew Chloe wouldn't do anything to harm Bre. But she had to be sick in the head if she thought I was letting this shit fly.

I swerved my car in front of the Cadillac truck Kristen was in and hopped out. She jumped out but wasn't nearly as quick as me. I made my way over to the driver's side and snatched the door open, pulling her security detail out. Hemming him up against the door, I held my arm against his neck and put my gun up to his temple.

"Where the fuck is my daughter?!"

"I don't know, man. I was just telling Kristen that I didn't see anything. She told me to park the car in the parking garage and come in after. I… I fell asleep in the car. I'm sorry, man."

"Antwon, baby, he doesn't know." Kristen grabbed at my hand, but I wasn't letting him loose. "Bae, put the gun away."

"Your fucking job was to keep watch and make sure they were safe. Am I right? Is that what I paid you to do?" I applied more pressure to his throat, and he was unable to respond with words, so he shook his head feverishly.

"Antwon, let him go!" Kristen's voice and the deep emotion in it made me release him. I turned to her, and her eyes were puffy and red from crying.

There was no doubt in my mind that she was sorry, but I was in no shape to console her. I didn't even have time to console my damn self. My only concern was finding Bre. Side stepping her, I tucked my gun in my waist and stormed inside Chloe's building. I didn't bother calling her phone. I knew for a fact that she wouldn't answer, throwing me further into a rage. That spare key that I had made came in handy. Without a second thought, I used the key to open the door.

"Bre… princess, you in here?" I called out while searching the house, and when I didn't get a response, I could no longer hold it together. "Fuckk!" I roared. "You fucking bitch, you fucking dirty ass bitch!" I felt like I was having an out of body experience as I picked up one of the lamps off the end table and launched it across the room.

"Antwon!" Kris shouted my name as I crumbled to the

floor. She kneeled down in front of me and put her forehead against mine. "Baby, I know. I know. We're gonna find her." In the moment, I was a shell of the man I had shown the world. Chloe had taken half of my heart. The only thing that was going to keep me going was knowing that Bre was alive. I had no doubt about that.

"I'ma kill that bitch, Kris. I'm going to fucking kill her!" Spit flew from my mouth, and I didn't give a fuck. Standing up, my eyes scanned the room, checking to see if anything in the house could possibly lead me to where Chloe had gone. Seeing nothing that stuck out, we left. Back downstairs, I sent the shaky security on his way, and Kris got in my car with me. "Tell me everything about today. From the time that you got to the theatre to the time they went missing."

While she gave me the run down, I drove to possible places Chloe could have gone. I even went by the law firm she worked at to see if she'd been in touch with anyone there. I wanted to drop Kris off, so I could beat the pavement, but she wasn't having it. My mind was so spaced out that I hadn't called my brother to let him know what had gone down. As I went to dial his number, my phone rang in my hand. Chloe's name flashed on the screen, and my body got hot. Kris looked at me and reached for the phone, but I had already answered and put it on speaker.

"Just tell me where my baby is." I kept my tone even. The last thing I wanted to do was convey my real feelings and make finding Bre even harder.

"As soon as you tell me where mine is." Kane's voice came through the line, and I gripped the steering wheel so tight my knuckles cracked.

"Ain't no kid of yours over here, you sick bastard!" Kris shrieked.

"Kristen, my love, you don't remember when we made that perfect little girl? You don't remember when my dick massaged your walls, and you begged me not to stop because it was so good?" He was getting a kick out of taunting her. Kris held her hand up to her mouth, and tears pooled in her eyes. I reached over and held onto her hand and mouthed that I had her.

"So, you help Chloe kidnap my child in hopes that it would give you some leverage? The only problem with that is Mackenzie isn't yours, and I know for a fact I'll be getting Bre back."

"That's where you're wrong, Antwon. Come to find out, Chloe had plans to take Bre all along. It just happened to work in my favor and here we are. I just hope when you do find us that you have my daughter with you, or yours won't make it." The line went dead.

Chloe

Being able to spend time with Bre was a breath of fresh air. To see my baby playing, laughing, wanting to be with me warmed my heart. It let me know that even though we were apart, she hadn't forgotten about me. The only downside was Kristen having to stand watch like I hadn't birthed this child. I tried my best to play nice since she was the reason for making the visits happen in the first place, but damn. It felt like she was breathing down my neck.

I went along with the arrangement for as long as I could, but that shit was getting real old real quick. No one seemed to respect the position I held in this co-parenting relationship. And I was over Ant making it seem like Kristen had more rights to my kid than me. So, I stayed quiet and plotted. Today was the day I'd put my plan in motion.

I made sure to pick the crowded theatre in Times Square for our movie date, knowing that it would be easy to get lost in the crowd. I only had one opportunity to get this right, so it had to work. Bre was coming home with me. Using the bathroom as my excuse to split off from Kristen worked perfectly with Bre actually having to use the bathroom.

"Okay, Bre'Ann, listen to Mommy. I'm going to take you to get some ice cream because Daddy is at work, okay?"

"Yayy! Kris coming too?"

"No!" I snapped, and she flinched. "I'm sorry, my baby." I silently cursed myself for my aggression. Gently rubbing her shoulders to let her know everything was okay, I continued. "No, Kristen can't come. She has to pick up your sister." She seemed satisfied with the answer, allowing me to take her hand in mine while we exited the bathroom.

Just when I thought I made it out safely, Kane's presence stuck a fork in the plan. Now, here we were on the expressway, going God knows where. I shook my head in disgust at the conversation he had with Ant. Alluding to possibly harming my child was worse than any pain he could've inflicted on me. But I would die before I let him hurt her.

"That baby is not yours, Kane. Kidnapping both me and my daughter is pointless."

"Watch ya words, Chloe." His warning went in one ear

and out the other. I was over backing down. I wasn't a docile woman when I met him, and at this point, I just didn't give a fuck.

"I'm not watching shit. I don't know if it's that shit you're putting up your nose or if you're just that blind. Kristen don't want you, and that baby, I'm sorry to tell you, boo, but she's a Brown." I snickered as he sat in the driver's seat, pondering. I knew he was trying to do the math and figure out if there was any truth to what I was saying. There was no need to. I had caught a glimpse of the baby, and I knew what I was talking about.

"You and I both know that if I wanted to, I could put your head through that window with no problem. I'm trying to be calm for the sake of your daughter in the backseat. Please just sit back and shut the fuck up."

I knew by the calmness in his tone that he was close to making good on his threat, and I didn't want Bre to see me get hit. I swallowed my next smart remark and started formulating a plan of escape, all while praying. Glancing in the rearview mirror, I caught Bre's eyes. She was quiet the whole time, staring straight ahead. Again, my selfishness had thrusted me into a fucked-up position, only this time, I'd gotten my baby caught up in it. If I didn't make it right, I wouldn't be able to live with myself.

WE HAD BEEN DRIVING SO LONG that I eventually fell asleep. When I awoke, we were still in the car, but it was no longer moving. We were parked in front of a house, and Kane was shoving the white powder up his nose while Bre stared at him with wide eyes.

"Are you fucking kidding me?! Bre, close your eyes, baby."

"I want my daddy!" she belted out before crying for the first time since we left the theatre. Kane tuned the both of us out, still snorting while I tried to console her.

"Shut that fucking kid up!" he vociferated, his voice only making her cry harder.

"Don't yell like that. She's just a fucking child!" I took off my seat belt and got out to tend to her. I didn't care about consequences. I may have wanted Bre with me, but not at the cost of being traumatized by Kane. "It's okay, Bre Bre, shhh. We're going to get ice cream soon, okay?"

"I gotta go pee," she said, wiping her tears with sadness still evident in her voice.

"Can we go somewhere, so I can take her to the bathroom?" I asked, trying my best to disguise my attitude. I could see him nodding off and yelled his name. "Kane!" I shoved his shoulder, jolting him awake.

"What?" he questioned, irritated and wide eyed like I had just disrupted his high.

"We have to use the bathroom."

"Aight, come on." Getting out, I held Bre in my arms and followed him up the worn steps and watched as he knocked on the door. He turned around quickly, pointing his finger in my face. "When we get inside, you keep your mouth shut."

"Where the hell are we?" I couldn't help but question.

"The last place anyone would think to look for us." That wasn't good at all. I wanted to ask another question, but the door opened up, and a man who looked like his twin stood on the other side of it.

"Yo' ass must be in some shit for you to drive all the way to Delaware to see me." The man's voice was gritty and deep. He had a menacing stare as he eyed the three of us.

"Delaware!" I shrieked, shocked that we were three hours outside of New York. A smack to my face caused me to stumble and Bre to bury her face into my chest, crying again. I knew my baby was scared, and I felt like shit for putting her in this predicament. I bit the inside of my cheek, wanting to cry out myself, but I couldn't fall apart.

"I taught you well, boy," the man said, praising Kane for his actions. "Come on in here." He held the door open for us to walk through, and my feet stayed planted.

Kane grabbed me by my arm, pulling me into the house. "Don't fucking embarrass me. The bathroom is to your left. I'll be waiting for you right here." He shoved me inside and locked the door behind us. I didn't want him to see I was scared, but on the inside, I was screaming for help.

"I'm okay, Bre. Stop crying, baby." I hugged her while helping her to use the bathroom.

"I want my daddy," she whispered with her head down.

Silently, I wanted him too. As I helped her wash her hands, I glanced down at my wrist, and my heart leaped out of my chest. I suddenly remembered that my Apple watch had a line that connected through my phone. My battery was on twenty percent, giving me more than enough juice to send a message to Kristen's phone.

Me: We're in Delaware. I'll text you when I get an address. Antwon needs to get here asap to get Bre.

Kristen: Are you with Kane?

The banging on the door scared the shit out of me.

Me: Yes, I gotta go. He's here.

"Let's go, Chloe."

"I'm coming out now. Okay, Bre, you hold Mommy's hand, okay? I promise I'm not gonna let anything happen to you, baby girl." I wiped her eyes and swallowed the lump in my throat before opening the door.

"What were you doing in there?"

"Making sure my daughter is good. She's scared." I turned up my nose, taking in the heavy cigarette smell.

"Come on." Hesitantly, I followed behind him, past the man, and into a room. I caught his smirk that made me uncomfortable, prompting me to pick Bre up again. Something wasn't right about him. "Sit." The room looked clean, but I was still hesitant to sit anywhere. Not wanting to start Kane up again, I sat in the rocking chair off in the corner.

"Hopefully in twenty-four hours, your baby daddy will call back, and we'll make the exchange."

"And if he doesn't?"

"I'll show you where China is." A chill went down my spine as he left out, closing the door behind himself. The look in his eyes said a lot.

"Don't worry, baby girl, Daddy will be here soon." Knowing that Ant would stop at nothing to ensure that no harm came to Bre was the only solace I had that we were getting out of this situation.

Kane

I didn't know why these women insisted on fucking with me. I had been trying to reach both Simone and Chloe on the phone for the past week or so, and they had been dodging me. While I was finally able to contact Simone, I wasn't so lucky with Chloe. I had been losing sleep and half my mind thinking about my daughter and Kristen. It felt like I was so close to getting them yet so far.

People didn't understand the love Kristen and I shared. Rather the love I had for her. She was nurturing from the moment I met her. She listened to me and was able to uncover the broken man I didn't know I was. Kristen taught me how to love her all the while holding me accountable for my actions. She didn't let me get away with just anything. As crazy as it sounded, I thought that I started putting my hands on her as a way to remind her that I was the man and leader in our household. I had Kristen's love, but I thrived off the fear.

When she finally got tired of that and left, I took advantage of the love that I knew China had for me. It didn't matter that I couldn't love her in the same capacity as Kristen. All that mattered was that she wanted to be there and allowed me the control I felt I needed. Just thinking about China made me want to weep, but no tears came. I had been by Ms. Doris' place to see Kristine but couldn't stay long.

Looking into her eyes was like looking at China. I couldn't be in her presence without thinking about what I had done to her mother. I assured Ms. Doris that I had someone looking into China's disappearance, and I was hopeful that I'd have some information soon. I hadn't updated her since then and had no plans on returning to her home.

Once Kristen was back with me and we had our daughter, we could start a new life. Both Chloe and Simone were two key pieces of making that a reality. I had driven past Chloe's apartment multiple times but didn't go upstairs. I didn't want to scare her into helping me, but as the days kept passing with her ignoring me, I became enraged, hence the reason I followed her to the theatre.

I waited outside, and when I saw her scurrying out hand

in hand with her daughter, I knew something was off. She kept looking behind her like she was running from something or someone. By the startled look on her face when she saw me, I knew she wished she'd rethought whatever plan she was attempting to execute. I snatched her up discreetly, and we were in the car on the way to a place I never thought I'd return to — my father's house. My father and I were estranged for more reasons than one, so I knew no one would think to look for me here.

It was the perfect set up for when I was ready to reach back out to Ant to set the exchange for Kristen and our baby. Everything would be on my terms. That bullshit Chloe was kicking about the baby not being mine didn't faze me because I knew better. I felt the moment I impregnated Kristen. She was mine.

Refocusing my attention as I sat across from the man that partially raised me, my high wore off. We had fallen out so many years ago that, in my mind, he was dead to me.

"We gonna sit here and stare at each other or you gonna tell me why you showed up here with a bitch and her bastard child?" he questioned, sounding like the same grouchy fucker he was when I was growing up.

"I won't be here long. Just needed somewhere to lay my head for the night then I'll be out of here."

"Oh, you think you gonna get off that easy? You running from something, and you brought that bullshit to my front door, so you gon' have to give me more than that." He sat down on the tattered couch and lit a cigarette.

"Tell me something about my mother."

"There's nothing to tell. She birthed you then left you. The end," he replied simply like that should have been enough to keep me from asking anything else. That answer, however, wasn't good enough for me.

"What would make her not want me? I didn't ask to be born, so I wanna know what made her make the conscious decision to not want to be my mother." I had thought about this plenty of times. Right now, it seemed like the best time to get those answers being that I didn't know what the outcome would be once Ant and I crossed paths. I wanted to get down to the bottom of this obsession I seemed to have with Kristen. Deep down, I felt like, in some way, she had some part of my mother I was longing for; I just couldn't put my finger on what it was.

"Don't ask me about that fucking woman anymore. She's dead to me, and she's dead to you! If you need to have a one on one with someone about your feelings, I suggest you find a fucking therapist!" he barked. His outburst didn't move me. I was my father's son; the apple didn't fall too far from the tree.

"There's this woman by the name of Kristen that I'm very much in love with. She knows my every flaw, down to the mommy issues that I developed growing up. Although I let her in, for some reason, I couldn't keep her. She was one of those women who didn't take my shit. You know, the kind of women you despise." He scoffed, and I continued. "My love for her didn't stop me from beating on her, which caused her to leave me. And then, there's China. You met her once. She loved me the same and stayed through the beatings, but our love couldn't hold a candle to what me and Kristen had. I'm here because I've been doing all I can to win her back. I've killed in the name of her love. I killed someone close to me."

My nose started to run, and it wasn't from the coke. I was crying. I was tapping into an emotion I never knew existed within me and doing so in front of a man who lacked an emotional compass and wasn't fond of empathy.

"So, you're blaming your life choices on not having a mother growing up? Where's my son, huh? ¿Dónde estás, Kane?" He asked where I was in Spanish. "I don't know who this punk is sitting in front of me." He took a pull of his cigarette and snorted. "Grow some fucking balls. Your mother made a decision not to be here. Tuck your tears in your back pocket and handle your shit like a man." That was his answer for everything — tuck your tears in your back pocket. I wasn't allowed to be in touch with my emotions growing up. Maybe that was the reason why it was so easy for me to detach myself emotionally from the things I did that I knew were wrong.

I shook my head at the old man my father became. He lived his life going from woman to woman and beating them into submission only to end up alone. He was part of the reason I had issues with women. I was never taught to respect them. I planned to be better once I got Kristen back. She was the only person between the heaven I could have with her or the hell I could rain down on the people she loved without her.

I turned to head back to the room where Chloe was and ran smack dead into her. Her hand was covering her mouth, and a distraught look covered her face. I stepped closer to her, and she moved backwards until she was up against the wall. I was sure she heard everything, but I wasn't admitting to anything.

"I knew it. I knew something was up." She spoke through her hand. "When I asked you about China, there was death in your tone when you responded." I stared silently, allowing her to make her own conclusion, still not admitting anything. "You... you killed her. You fucking killed your own child's mother, you sick bastard!" she yelled out.

I closed the space between us and placed my hands on her shoulders, squeezing them tightly. "Listen to me. Whatever you think you heard, you didn't. If I hear you speak on it again, I can't be responsible for how I react. Do you understand me?" She nodded rapidly. "No, I need to hear that you understand me. It could make a difference between my life and your death."

"Yes."

"Couldn't have been me. I would've put her head right

through that wall," my father commented from where he was still sitting.

"It's late, and you're going to need your rest for tomorrow. You can lay with your daughter in the bed, and I'll sleep in the rocking chair." I guided her back to the room with my hand on the small of her back. Her shoulders dropped, and she hung her head.

"Kane, just let us go. I won't tell Ant where you are. Let me just take my daughter and get out of town please," she begged.

Looking into her eyes, I said the first thing that came to mind. "It's above me now."

Kaia

"Come on, Maine, pick up the fucking phone. Now is not the time for this shit." I talked to the phone as I dialed Maine's number for the fifth time since hanging up with my sister.

To find out that Chloe had taken Bre, only to turn around and get them both snatched up by Kane, had to be the craziest shit I'd ever heard. I was pissed off and nervous at the same time. I was pissed that Kane was actually able to pull it off and scared that Bre had to be in the presence of that psycho. My heart went out to Ant and my sister, knowing they were both going crazy trying to track Chloe down. I knew Kristen was beating herself up for her push to keep Bre close to her mother. Her good deed had blown up in her face.

Hopping up from my bed, I threw on a Champion sweatsuit and pulled my hair up into a ponytail. Packing Kymani a quick bag, I picked her up and got her dressed. Ma Jane had Chase overnight, so I was going to drop Mani off at my parents' house. With Bre missing, we needed all hands on deck, and I wanted to be useful in any way I could, even if it was just for emotional support. Leaving the house, I threw Mani's bag in the back, strapped her into her car seat, and hopped in the driver's side. Pulling my phone from my hoodie, I attempted to call Maine again, only for the call to go to voicemail.

I hadn't heard from him since this morning when he left for the studio. He had a habit of putting his phone on silent whenever he was there. I fussed with him about it all the time, expressing the importance of having the phone available at all times, especially in the case of an emergency. This right now was an emergency, and the fact that I couldn't get him on the line was frustrating me to no end. It was bad enough that Bre had been gone for hours. I didn't need another thing to worry about.

All kinds of smoke signals went off in my head. We had gotten into it again, with the source of the argument being Simone. Though I tried to shake the ill feeling I had in my gut about her for the sake of keeping peace within my relationship, I couldn't. That bitch was no good. And my calls going unanswered wasn't looking good for him. Instead of harping on that, I pushed forward to my parents' house.

"Excuse me, Kaia Phillips?" I heard my name called, prompting me to look up as I grabbed Kymani's car seat and baby bag. A man in an overly starched suit approached me with his hand out. "Here, let me help you with that."

"Umm, no, I can manage. How can I help you?" I stepped back and closed the door.

"My name is Detective Pierce. I'm here about Kandice Thompson. Did you know she was missing?"

I kept my face straight and answered. "No, I didn't. Should I have?"

"Well, seeing as you are with her child's father, I would think that you'd want to be aware. Just in case it affected you in the long run, if you know what I mean."

"Actually, I don't. If you'll excuse me, I need to get my daughter inside. I have a pressing family matter that needs my attention." I kept the conversation short. The more you talked, the more the police tried to trip you up. I wasn't going for it.

"Well," he kissed his teeth sarcastically, "this missing person's case may actually be a murder, so I'm sure whatever it is you have going on can wait. What do you think?" I frowned, wanting so badly to curse his ass out and wipe the smug look off his face, but decided to keep my cool. "I'll wait while you get your baby settled."

I stomped upstairs, pissed that I even had to deal with this shit. The door swung open just as I went to take my key out of my pocket. Kris stood on the other side of it with heavy, sleep deprived eyes.

"What are you doing here, Kaia? I told you to stay home with the baby, and I'd keep you posted." She sniffled as fresh tears spilled over the dry streaks on her face.

"And I told you Bre is my niece, and I wasn't going to sit at home. twiddling my thumbs, waiting for y'all to call me with updates." I walked past her, and she still had the door open.

"Who's that man looking like the police standing outside?"

"He is the police. Close the door." She did as I instructed and stood against it. "Where everybody at?"

"Mommy in the room, putting Kenzie down for a nap, and Dad left out behind Ant. I fucked up bad, Kaia. I wasn't paying attention, and she.... she just took her. Right from under my nose, she took her." I pulled her in for a hug while making sure to leave space for Kymani.

"I know, sis. It's okay. We gonna get her back and not a hair on her head will be outta place." I assured her, giving all the hope I could. "Look, I need you to watch Mani for me for a few. I have to go down to the precinct with this detective."

"Wait. Precinct? For what?"

"Something about Kandice being missing and him

wanting to ask me questions. We both know I don't know shit, so I should be in and out of there."

"Hold on, where the hell is Maine? And when the hell did Kandice go missing? This is some extra shit we don't need. I just need to be focused on getting Bre back."

"And trust me, we're on the same page with that, but this dude showing up here ain't no coincidence." She nodded in agreeance. "Let me go down there and see what he's talking about. And Maine... I don't even know, Kris."

I handed her the baby and told her to text me if she heard anything else about Bre. Back outside, the detective was in the same place I'd left him, only now he was leaning up against my car like he paid the note. I really didn't know where Kandice had disappeared to, nor did I care. The last time I saw her, I whipped her ass, and Maine revoked her parental rights after she basically said fuck her own son.

Since then, Maine hadn't brought her up once. Chase wasn't hurting for nothing, so for me, there was no reason to question her whereabouts. I just wished that Maine was around to give me something so that I wouldn't be going into this precinct blindsided. He never once mentioned what happened during his questioning, and at this point, I had nothing to go on.

"If you'd like, you can ride in my car. It doesn't have all those sirens and lights on it. I'd hate to make you look or feel like you've committed a crime." There was that smug grin again.

"No thanks. I'd much rather drive my own car. That's going to require you getting off it. Can we make this quick? As I said, I have a family emergency."

"I won't hold you long. We're gonna head to the thirteenth precinct." I waited until he got in his car and pulled off before I got ready to take a different route to get there. Unlocking my phone, I sent Maine a text.

My Love: I don't know if I have to send a smoke signal to let you know when there's an emergency, but right about now, we have another 911 situation. If you don't hit me back within the hour, I'm coming to find you.

I sent the message with a nagging feeling in my heart that if I had to go looking for Maine, I wasn't going to like what I found. I made it to the precinct, and Detective Pain In The Ass — a.k.a. Pierce — stood out front like he was making sure I showed up.

"It's really that serious, huh?" He motioned with his hand to escort me inside once I got out of the car. I walked in, and all eyes were on me. For some reason, all the so-called police work had stopped for them to focus on me. For me not to be a suspect, I damn sure was starting to feel like one.

"Follow me, Ms. Phillips," Detective Pierce instructed.

I followed, making sure to stay aware of my surroundings. There had been too many Black people not making it out of the police station after going in willingly. I wanted to walk out the same way I came in. When I walked through the building, the atmosphere didn't feel as heavy as it was in what I assumed was the interrogation room. I felt anxious and hoped that my face didn't show it.

"So, Ms. Phillips, can you tell me the last time you had contact with the victim?"

"Oh, so she's a victim now? I thought she was a missing person." I caught onto his ulterior motive, and he knew it.

"Well, once a person has been missing a certain number of days, in this case more than a month, our assumption is there's some type of foul play."

"Damn, that's not how I remember it on *Law & Order*, but who am I to dictate the rules?" I could tell I was getting under his skin while trying to figure out the best way to answer the question. "Back to your question though, the last time I was in contact with Kandice was over a month ago. My boyfriend and I went over to her house to pick up his son."

"Did the two of you have at it while you were there?"

My eyebrows raised in confusion. "Have at it?" I asked, seeking clarification.

"As in argue. Did you two argue about anything?"

"Oh, no. We don't have anything to argue about. She's not too fond of me, and I'm not her biggest fan either, so I don't waste my time exchanging words with her." I glanced at my watch to see if there were any messages from Kristen or Maine. Seeing nothing from either of them, I focused back on the detective.

"Hmm, okay. Did your boyfriend have any problems with

her? You know, any baby mama drama?" He used air quotes and did some stupid ass head movement.

"You do know that not all Black people have baby mama/baby daddy drama, right?" I threw the air quotes back at him. "Look, good luck on finding her but this is a waste of my time." I went to stand and made my way to the door.

"You're free to go, Ms. Phillips. Please don't schedule any vacations and be sure to let Mr. Brown know not to take that tour bus too far. I'm sure we'll be seeing each other real soon." There was a threat in his tone, but that didn't stop me from walking out of the room.

I pulled out my phone and smashed the keys on my keyboard, texting Maine. I was so fed up I didn't know what to do. Occasionally looking up to watch where I was going so not to make the mistake of bumping into anyone, my eyes met those of Kandice's mom. She was seated on a bench near the exit with a scowl etched on her face.

I didn't need to be seen arguing with this girl's mother, especially after being questioned about her disappearance. So, I kept it moving to my car and hoped to get there without incident.

"Hey, hey, you. Kaia, right? Yeah, I remember you. You the girl that had beef with Kandice, and now you're with her ex, trying to raise my grandbaby!" She pointed, shouting while inching closer to my car. "I know he has something to do with my daughter being missing. And y'all kidnapped my grandbaby." I went to my voice memos and hit record because she was talking crazy, and there was no telling what else she was capable of.

"Ms. Thompson, I don't know what you're talking about, and I would appreciate it if you moved away from my car." I was trying not to disrespect my elders, but she was about to make me take it there.

"Girl, tell me anything. The only way I'm going away is if the big superstar pays me. I need a hunnit Gs by the end of the week, or I'ma tell it on the mountain, over the hills and everywhere." She motioned with her fingers, thumbing imaginary money. "Play with it if y'all want to," she threatened before turning on her heels and walking back into the precinct.

Stopping the recording, I watched her waddle off with my mouth open. This bitch didn't give a damn about her daughter or grandson. She wanted to see how she could come up off Maine. As I stood there, stuck in my thoughts, my phone rang, and Maine's name flashed across the screen.

"**Where the hell are you, Tremaine?!**" I barked into the phone.

"**Ughh, Maine, this dick is so good, Daddy,**" a female's voice cried out, stunning me to silence. My heart sank to my feet, and I couldn't get a word out before the call disconnected. My mind went blank, and all I could see was flashes of me on the eleven o'clock news for killing this motherfucka.

Using the tracking app we had installed on our phones in case of emergencies, I let my GPS guide me to Maine's location, the Hyatt Regency in Jersey City. I hadn't had to use it until now, and to know what I was using it for had me heated. I didn't know how I managed to drive to the address in the state that I was in, but by the grace of God, I made it in one piece. I sat in my car, thinking about all the different ways I could blow this bitch up with Maine in it and get away scot-free. None of my ideas ended in a happy ending, so I had to improvise.

"Hi, I'm looking for my boyfriend. He called me to pick him up, and it sounded like he was in trouble." I spoke to the fair skinned woman at the front desk. "Can you tell me if this man is in one of your rooms? I tracked his phone here." I flashed a picture of Maine, and her eyes lit up in recognition before she tried to straighten her facial expression.

"I'm sorry, ma'am. Unfortunately, I can't give out any guest information."

"No, you don't understand. My boyfriend is a rapper with Promise Records. If I call the media, there will be a circus so big outside of this hotel, you wouldn't know what hit you. Do you want bad press for this beautiful hotel?" She shook her head no. "I didn't think so. Now, all I need is a key to his room, and we can forget this conversation ever happened."

She handed me the key quickly, and I thanked her while walking in the direction of the elevators like I owned the place. "He's with the singer!" she shouted out as the elevator doors opened, and I stepped in. She only confirmed what I knew.

Maine

Me: Yo, we need to chop it up. You free today?

I texted Simone as I left the house after another heated argument with Kaia. I wasn't beat for arguing, especially about the same shit over and over. Unfortunately for me, that had been the case between Kaia and I. Somehow, the name Simone shook up the atmosphere in my crib, and I wasn't feeling that shit. Shouldn't no woman have the ability to have my woman in her feelings concerning me. I belonged to Kaia and vice versa.

Simone B: Yeah, I'm just leaving my yoga class. I'll give you the address to where you can meet me.

She answered back immediately like I figured she would. This conversation with Simone was long overdue for mine and her sake. I walked out on Kaia in the middle of her barking about yet another text from Simone. Now, I could admit that she had been texting me more than before since hitting my car, but I didn't think anything of it. According to Kaia, that was the problem.

I didn't look too much into the shit Simone did because I wasn't checking for her. I thought it was a good thing, but it turned out that it only made me look more suspect. When I put the address into my GPS that she'd given me, I didn't expect to be pulling into the parking lot of a hotel. Still, I pushed forward. Stepping off the elevator in the hotel, I felt something pulling me back and telling me to retreat. And normally I listened to my gut, but thinking about the tension in my household, this shit couldn't go on another day.

I pushed the nagging feeling to the side and kept it pushing toward her room. I knocked, and when she came to the door, I did a double take. She had on what looked like a pair of men's sweatpants and an oversized t-shirt. I was taken aback because I was used to her being done up and in something fitted. The look actually showed her natural beauty. And I wasn't looking like a nigga that wanted her. I just found it attractive that she knew how to tone it down a little. That was what made Kaia so sexy. My shorty could rock a heel or a sneaker and still put bitches to shame.

"I know you didn't come all the way here to talk to me from the hallway."

"Well, you didn't invite me in. Niggas done got jammed up for less."

"This is true, but you're good here. Come on in." She motioned with her hand, and I walked in and stood not too far from the door. "Have a seat. What'd you wanna talk about?" She sat in the dining area, awaiting my response.

"Your behavior."

"My behavior?" she said, with her finger pointed at herself.

"Yeah, man. These text messages, the flirting, and shit. You causing confusion in my household." I didn't know how else to word it without being straight up about it.

"I don't do anything that you don't allow me to do."

"What you mean by that?"

She stood and made her way over to me. Leaving just enough respectable space between the two of us, she rested her hand on her hip. "I mean, you never say stop texting you. I don't recall you checking me about the flirting either. It's okay to secretly want me just as bad as I want you." She said that shit like it was the gospel. My head cocked to the side, allowing her words to sink in my head.

"So, that's how you interpret if somebody wants you?" I had to make sure I was hearing her right.

"Yep." I couldn't hold it in anymore. I held my hand to my mouth and burst out laughing.

"Girl, if you don't get outta here with that junior high school shit." Her lips pursed like she was eating something sour. "Yo, I'm sorry to laugh, but it's really not like that. There's no denying that you're a great person, and I'm sure you'd make someone happy, but I already have that."

"With who? Kaia? How could you have that with her and have had a baby with someone else?" She smirked like she had one up on me or had said some fly shit that wasn't already known.

"I didn't have a baby on Kaia. Chase was conceived before we got together. Man, let me go cause I see you tryna be messy and I don't play female games. And had you met me before Kaia, I would've hurt your feelings on GP. I just ask that you respect the boundary I'm setting, or we can't make music together." She stopped me as I went to make my exit.

"Okay, you got it. I'll check my feelings and respect the boundary." I turned my head, and her face showed that it pained her to say those few words. "Since you're here, you wanna hang back a little and listen to this track I made? I promise you're gonna love it."

"Nah, we gon' have to do that at the studio. I took a risk by coming here in the first place. If Kaia even thought up this scenario, she'd murk my Black ass. And I don't know about you, but I'm a gift to this world and don't plan on leaving it no time soon."

"Aww, come on, just for an hour max. I got some Kool-

Aid, and I can make a mean chicken salad sandwich. On some friend shit for real. I really value your opinion."

"Aight, an hour, Simone." She smiled and headed to the kitchen. She returned only five minutes later with the food and drinks. "Damn, you already had this prepared?" I asked suspiciously.

"The chicken salad, yeah, so it didn't take too much to put it together. Here's your cup. I'ma grab my phone so I can play the song for you." I examined the cups, making sure they both had the same amount of juice before swapping them.

Returning with her phone in hand and a big smile, she sat down and played the track. One track turned into two, and I had finished my drink along with the sandwich. It was good as hell too.

"So, what you think?" I heard her say. My head felt like it was spinning. *What the fuck is going on?* "Maine, did you hear what I said about the remix?"

"What the fuck you put in my drink, Simone?"

"Something to make you relax. You seem so tense." I stood up to leave, and my legs felt like they would give out at any moment. "Uh oh, be careful. Here, let me help you lay down." I snatched my arm from her and ended up falling on my ass.

"Ughh, Maine, this dick is so good." I heard Simone's voice, but she wasn't next to me. I didn't know how I got on this couch or when I fell asleep, but I felt disoriented when I got up. All I could think about was wrapping my hands around

this bitch's neck and strangling the fuck out of her. I marched toward her voice, halting only when I heard her on the phone.

"Yes, I did what you asked me to do, and I'm done with this shit!" She snapped on whoever was on the other end of the phone. **"Kane, release the damn tape. I don't give a fuck no more. After they find out I drugged Maine, it's over for my career anyway."**

"So, you been plotting with this nigga the whole time?" I made my presence known, and she jumped, making the phone slip from her hand, hitting the floor. "Oh, what, you thought that shit you put in my drink was gon' have my ass out for the count, huh?" I moved stealthily toward her, and she walked backwards with her hands up.

"Maine, you don't understand. Kane made me do all this shit. I was in a fucked-up situation. I trusted him, my family, to hold me down, and all he did was suck me into the shit he has going on." She was copping all types of pleas that fell on deaf ears.

"You been watching us for this nigga? You know all the fucked-up shit that's been happening! Wait, you were the one who told him about Kenzie at the hospital." As I came to the realization, I upped my nine and pointed it at the center of her head. "Tell me every-fucking-thing he got going on. I mean every fucking detail."

The thought of her life becoming a memory made her do the right thing and start talking. By the time she was done, I was astounded by how much Kane was able to pull off using the people that surrounded us. After hearing about Kandice's involvement, I was happy I got rid of that hoe.

"Who were you talking to on the phone before?" I asked, referring to her fake ass acting like I was fucking her. She put her head down.

"Kaia. She had been calling your phone back-to-back, and I returned the call."

"Fuck!" I knew this shit was going to blow up in my face.

"Oh, y'all real fucking bold. Real, real fucking bold." Kaia's voice made my body cold. I didn't even want to turn around. I hoped for my sake that she could see me fully dressed and look past what her eyes saw.

"Kaia, I…" Simone couldn't articulate the rest of her sentence before Kaia ran up and hit her with a closed fist.

"Bitch, I told you I was gon' dog walk yo' ass, didn't I?" Kaia growled, hitting Simone with combos, not giving her a chance to recover. I let it go on for a few minutes because every hit was well deserved.

"Aight, bae, let her go." I tried pulling her off Simone, only for her to swing on me. "Whoa, chill the fuck out!" I grabbed at her hand after she caught me good on the side of my head.

"Chill my fuckin' ass. While you over here kekeing with this bitch, our fucking niece is gone. Bring yo' ass on," she seethed before kicking Simone, who was now balled up in a fetal position. "Bitch, if I ever see your fucking face again, I'ma make you regret it more than you do now."

She grilled me and walked out. I put my gun away and let Simone know she could consider her contract with the label scrapped. Grabbing my phone from the table, I left out and found Kaia waiting at the elevator. She didn't even acknowledge my presence as she pressed the elevator button aggressively.

"Babe, that shit wasn't what it looked like." I regretted the common line of a serial cheater as soon as it left my lips.

"It looked like you were in the hotel of the same bitch I specifically asked you to be cautious of. Were you not just in there?" She still hadn't turned to look at me.

"Yeah, but..."

"That's just it, Maine, there's no fucking but. Look, let's just get to my parents' house so we can see if there's any updates on Bre's whereabouts." I felt like shit. I had been out the loop for the last few hours, and my brother needed me. With all that Simone had divulged, she had to be dealt with.

Ant

I hadn't slept in the last twenty-four hours. I felt like it wasn't okay for me to rest with Bre missing. I didn't care how much sleep I lost. I had to find my little girl. I hadn't seen Kristen since I dropped her off at her parents' place, and right now, it felt like it was best that we were apart for the moment. I wanted to say that I wasn't holding her responsible for Bre being gone, but in a way, I was. If it wasn't for her suggesting that Bre see her snake ass mama, my baby would be home where she belonged. I'd been at my mom's house after scouring the streets and looking up under every rock I thought Chloe or Kane could be under only to find nothing.

"Antwon, here, baby, take this phone," my mother said, handing me her house phone. I'd been sitting in the same spot since last night after another failed search. I didn't want to be home if my baby girl wasn't there.

"Ma, I don't feel like talking to nobody right now. I'm trying to figure some shit out." I waved off the phone and answered a text message from my private investigator. She had been digging deeper into Kane's background to see if he had family out of town or anything. So far, she had one hit on his father, but we were waiting on verification. This clown thought I would exchange one daughter for the other. The only thing I had for him in exchange for Bre was a bullet to the head.

"Well, it's a good thing she's not nobody. Here, it's Kristen." I shook my head no. I wasn't in the right frame of mind to deal with her. She had been on an apologizing spree, leaving voice messages and texts, crying and apologizing. An apology wasn't going to get Bre back. Me being in these streets and not wasting time on the phone with her was. **"He wants me to tell you he's not here."** I shot my mother a hard look and shook my head. She was foul for that. **"Okay, baby, alright, bye."**

"Now why you had to go say all that?"

"Say all what? What you afraid to say? You can't ignore that girl like that. Did you forget that she's going through it like you? Imagine how she feels like she let you down after encouraging this whole thing. She's beating herself up enough while still trying to be a mother to Kenzie, be there for you, and find Bre."

I stood up, irritated that she was trying to defend Kristen at a time like this. "Yo, Ma, on some real shit, she should be blaming herself." There, I had finally said how I truly felt. "I was adamantly against this because I had a gut feeling some shit was gonna go left. And I always trust my gut, always, Ma. It seems like I've been leading it instead of letting it lead me."

"And I'm not saying you're wrong about how you feel, Antwon, but you're going about it in the wrong way. That energy you have needs to be pointed at that slick bitch, Chloe. You know Kristen meant well and had no way of knowing that Chloe would try to kidnap her own child or get caught up with that son of a bitch, Kane. Nobody could've predicted that, son." She was right, but I really wasn't trying to hear it. The fact still remained that my daughter went missing on her watch.

I heard keys in the door, and when I turned to face it, Maine was walking in. I hadn't put him on to anything or anyone for that matter. If he knew what was going on, it was through Kristen telling Kaia. He walked past my mother and over to me, pulling me into a brotherly embrace. I hugged him back, patting his back with my fist and trying to dismiss the tightening in my chest. There was no time to cry. I would cry once I was reunited with my little girl.

"I'm sorry, bro. I'm just now finding shit out. And that's my bad. I haven't been on my A game. What's the move?" He got right to it, and that was all I needed. My mom left us to ourselves.

"Man, I've been in the streets looking everywhere, and niggas acting like they don't know nothing. I even hit Ross again, and he can't tell me nothing. I'm waiting for my P.I. to come through on her end with some info."

"Yo, you ain't gon' believe what I found out today from Simone."

"Simone?" I asked with a raised brow.

"Yeah. Once we get Bre back, I can give you more detail about that. Check this though. Remember when we both said someone around us gotta be feeding information to Kane for him to know our moves?" I nodded. "Yeah, well, turns out that Simone is that source."

"Nah, ain't no way, bro," I said in disbelief.

"I heard it from her directly, bro. Even heard her on the phone with the nigga. That's her cousin, her blood cousin." I sat back and put two and two together in my mind. It didn't take long to figure it out. "Yeah, man, I almost made her disappear like I did Kandice, but I have something else in store for her ass."

"This nigga was really recruiting the women to dismantle us, man. We look crazy as hell, Maine. And now he got my baby. Ahhh, man."

"We gon' find her. I promise you the sun won't set without us having Bre back."

"I can't have it any other way, my nigga. One hour is too

long. She's been gone now for a whole twenty-four. I'm really starting to regret pursuing Kris, man. It pains me to say that, but I didn't have none of these problems until we got together. And don't get me wrong, I love the shit out of her. She bore my seed and treats Bre like her own, but I don't know if I can stay if I don't get Bre'Ann back." The words sounded foreign leaving my mouth. Maine hit my arm and signaled with his head toward the hallway. My heart broke more seeing Kristen standing there with Kenzie strapped to her chest and tears coming down her cheeks.

"I can't tell you enough how sorry I am, Antwon. I can admit that I failed Bre and you too. I just came by to give you this info." She walked over and put a piece of paper on the table in front of me. "Chloe reached out and let me know that Kane had them out at some house in Delaware. Heaven's husband, Dre, works for an IT company, and he was able to track her through her Apple I.D. to this address. Please tell Bre that I love her so much and I'm sorry."

She walked out, leaving me no room to say anything in response. I was too focused on the paper in front of me anyway. While looking over the address, my phone buzzed, and it was the P.I. She had sent me an address, and it matched the one on the paper.

"Bro, I got this nigga." I got up and headed for the door. I would address Kristen as soon as I was back with Bre. Right now, it was time to put an ending to this shit.

THE GPS ESTIMATED a three-hour drive to Delaware, but I pushed my Aston Martin to the limit to make it two. No music played; I wanted silence. I needed to be able to hear my own thoughts. As my mind formulated different ways to kill Kane, I didn't think about my record label nor jail time. I was going to murk this nigga, and that was all there was to it.

"Bro, pull up right here. This the address," Maine said as he watched the GPS.

The old house looked like it had seen better days, but I wasn't here for redecorating anything other than Kane's face. Quite frankly, whoever opened the door and didn't have the information I was seeking would get it too. Screwing my silencer onto my gun, I jumped out the car with Maine falling in step at my side. I nodded for him to knock on the door.

"I hope you not back here with more questions because I ain't got shit for you," a grumpy man said from behind the door before opening it slightly. Not with the shits, I pushed it hard, hitting him in the face. "Arghh, shit."

"Now, sir, I usually respect my elders, but today, I'm not feeling like that. Where the fuck is Kane?!" I barked.

"I don't know. The boy left here last night with a woman and a little girl. He didn't tell me where he was going," he responded with his chest poked out like he wanted smoke. I knocked him right in his shit, and he hit the wall. This was not the time to play the loyalty game. "Alright, alright, they're at the Red Roof Inn motel. It's twenty minutes from here."

Pfft, pfft, pfft. The bullets from Maine's silencer went into dude's body at rapid succession.

I looked over at him, and he shrugged his shoulders. "Anything connected to that bitch ass nigga is outta here," he declared before we left out the same way we came in.

PULLING in front of the motel, I knew we needed to get in and get out. It looked like a scene from a movie. The rooms were set up outside, and there was heavy traffic around the place. By the seedy neighborhood we were in, I knew why Kane chose it. It was the perfect spot to lay low in, and I knew no one would care about our status. We didn't get a chance to get the room number, so we sat in the parking lot a few minutes, trying to figure out the best way to go about getting the info. It was a good thing we kept still too because I spotted Kane coming out of the last room on the first floor.

It was ducked off, and the light was out under the steps. It was clear that he thought he was safe in the area because he wasn't trying to hide his face as he proceeded to walk over to a group of guys who I could tell were working the block. Watching the exchange of money from one hand to another, I had a strong feeling that his drug of choice was coke. It had to be the way he was moving about life.

"That nigga out here down bad." Maine pointed out.

"Not for long." I waited until he went back in the room and gestured for Maine to get out of the car. We both tossed our hoodies over our heads in case the people in the vicinity didn't carry the same no snitch policy that we did. Leaning against the door frame, I listened for any signs of Bre or Chloe and gritted my teeth when I heard Bre crying.

"Why the hell she keep crying like that?!" I heard Kane yell.

"I told you she was burning up. She's not fucking feeling well, and all you care about is getting high," Chloe retorted. Hearing that my baby was sick, I no longer wanted to prolong the inevitable.

"And I keep telling you to watch your fucking mouth!" **WHAP!** I heard the sound of Chloe being struck through the door.

I got ready to kick the door in, and Maine stopped me. "Wait, bro, that nigga high off that shit. If we go kicking down the door, ain't no telling what he might do."

"My nigga, do you hear my baby in there?" I gritted with wild eyes.

"Bro, trust me. Gimme a minute." He walked off, leaving me standing guard at the door. When he returned, he had the dude with him that made the exchange with Kane.

"Dude says Kane copped from him a couple times since last night. And he saw Bre once through the window."

"Yeah, man, I could tell duke was a little off. Had I known

he was on bullshit, I would've popped his ass myself. This my shit here." He pointed to the perimeter of the motel. "Do what you gotta do. Ain't nobody gon' say nothing."

"Good looking. I need to get in there though."

"Say no more." He went around me and knocked at the door. Maine and I stood out of eyesight in the darkness.

"Who is it?"

"Yo, it's Tron. I got something I want you to test for me. Big boy shit compared to what I just gave you." The lock on the door popped, and Kane poked his head out.

"Where is it?" he inquired.

The built-up rage inside of me snapped. I grabbed him by his throat and forced him back into the room. His eyes widened, and he tried to talk, but my grip was so tight that no words would come out.

"Bitch ass nigga, you didn't think I'd find you, did you?" I took my fist, and it collided with his eye. I commenced to beating the shit out of him for Kristen, me, Mecca, and whoever else he fucked over. I stomped all over his body and his head.

"Daddy!" I heard Bre call out, but I couldn't stop. "Daddy!" she screamed again.

Sending a vicious kick to Kane's limp body, I stepped back. I didn't get a chance to turn around fully before she ran to me. My hands were swollen, and Kane's blood had splattered all over my clothes, but it didn't stop me from swooping Bre up in my arms. I held her tight as she cried. Glancing over her shoulder, I glared at Chloe, whose left eye was swollen shut. She diverted her good eye from me and looked toward the door. Ignoring everybody in the room, including Kane, who was laid out unconscious, I walked out. I knew that Maine would handle the rest.

"Bre'Ann, Daddy loves you so much, and I'm so sorry that this happened. Did that man hurt you? Did Mommy hurt you?" I didn't really know the woman I'd laid down and bore a child with, and at this juncture, I couldn't put anything past her.

"No, Daddy. The bad man hit Mommy hard, and she cry." Her little chest started to heave up and down as she cried. I rubbed her back in a circular motion to calm her down. "Daddy, I don't feel good."

"Okay, baby girl. We going home, so Daddy can give you some medicine." I looked out the window and saw Maine coming toward us with Chloe bringing up the rear. "You handled that?" He only nodded in confirmation.

"He'll be unrecognizable when they find him. Uncle love you, Bre Bre," he said to Bre, who had fallen asleep. "I'll drive, bro." I got out and went to get in the backseat. I wasn't trying to let Bre go anyway. I watched Chloe stand outside the car as Maine put it in drive. I wanted so badly to put a bullet in her head and leave her body right there, but I didn't. I planned to handle her once we were back in our jurisdiction.

"Get in," I said to her. She didn't attempt to get in the

backseat, and that was smart on her part. While we drove, I pulled out my phone and texted Kristen and my mama. Kristen responded first.

Me: We found her, and I'm headed back to the crib. Can you meet me there?

Bae: (praying hand emoji) thank God. Umm, I think she should spend tonight with you. I'll swing by tomorrow, cool?

Me: Cool.

The ride back to the city was longer than our ride here, but I was okay with that. As long as my little girl was in my arms, everything was good. Kane's soul was on its way to hell, and all was right with the world. Simone would be seeing me as soon as I got my family back on track. We pulled up to Chloe's apartment, and she looked back to me and spoke.

"Antwon, I know what I did was unforgivable. I just need you to know that I love that little girl very much. I did what I felt I had to do in order to have some kind of authority as a parent. A parent, Antwon. You do understand that I'm one just like you. And no, I don't make all the right decisions, but when it comes to her, I do my damned best to. All I ask is that you start taking that into consideration."

If it wasn't for the many stupid decisions that she made that had put our child in danger on countless occasions, I probably would've believed her. With what had transpired, the thin line of trust I had left was nonexistent.

"Chloe, hear me clear when I say this because it'll be the last time you'll ever hear my voice for a while. You're **dead** to me. A fuckin' corpse. What I really wanna do to you, God wouldn't be pleased with me for even thinking it. Please do yourself a favor and stay the fuck outta my way. You'll be hearing from my lawyer soon regarding custody." I tapped the back of Maine's headrest, and he pulled off.

Kristen

When I got the text from Ant that he had Bre, my heart felt at ease. Instead of being at the house when she made it back home, I gave him space to get her settled. I had been beating myself up the whole time she was gone. I could admit that I had dropped the ball in a major way. I let my kindness over-shadow my common sense. Walking in on Ant confirming my suspicions that he blamed me for what happened also crushed me.

I couldn't argue with the fact that I had unknowingly

brought my Kane baggage into our relationship, but to hear him express his regret for pursuing me stung a bit. I wasn't sure where our relationship would go from here or if there was even a relationship. I put it to the back of my mind temporarily. Right now, I was getting Kenzie together so that we could go see him and love up on Bre. I'd made the decision to stay with my parents until I figured out whether or not I would be moving back to my place. With Kane no longer being an issue, it didn't sound like a bad idea.

"Hey, where you headed to?" Kaia asked from where she was sitting in the living room, nursing Kymani. She had returned home too but had yet to tell me why.

"I'm going over to Ant's house to see Bre for a little bit. What you doing today?"

"Just school and food shopping later. I think Mommy tryna starve us out, so we can go back to our men." I had to laugh because she was lowkey right. I'd never seen my mother's fridge as bare as it had been lately.

"I'll be glad when y'all catch on and go head. Not my babies though." My mom came from the back of the house and kissed Kenzie's head and took Kymani from Kaia's arms to burp her.

"Dang, Ma, that's how you really feel?"

"You know I'm just playing; I love having you girls here, and you know my grands are my everything." I felt a but coming on. "I just know you two aren't in a good place with your other halves. I need y'all to fix that. Now that the Kane mess is put to rest, we need to get everything and everyone back on one accord. Ain't that right, Munchie Munch?" she cooed at Kymani.

"How do we patch things up after all of this?" Kaia inquired with a long face.

"Yeah," I added. "Starting to feel like love can't even keep us together because something or someone is always fighting against us."

"Do you love Antwon, Kristen?"

"Of course I do, Ma. You know that, he knows that, everyone knows that."

"And do you love Tremaine, Kaia?"

Kaia sighed. "With all my heart."

"Then it sounds like it's worth fighting for to me. Ain't no way y'all let God send you the right men, all for you to let these devils take them from you. Yes, this family has been tested left and right, but we made it through. And the reason why I can encourage you both to go back home is because I looked those guys in their eyes when they professed their love for y'all. It's rare, and you can't fake it. Trust me when I tell you."

Arriving at Ant's house, I knocked on the door instead of using my key like I normally would. It may have been petty of me, but for right now, that was where we were. When he opened the door, my heart and my clit didn't miss a beat as they reacted to his presence. I had Kenzie in her car seat still, and he reached for it with a big smile.

"Hey, Daddy's baby. I missed you, Kenzie girl." I let him grab the seat and walked in behind him, closing the door.

"Daddy, who here?" Bre asked from wherever she was before making her appearance from the back of the house just as we walked in

"I'm here," I announced, laughing as she ran to me.

"Krissss, I missed you!"

"Aww, I missed you too, mamas." I couldn't help but tear up a little at how things could've gone left if she wasn't found. "I love you, Bre'Ann."

"I love you too, Kris. Can you put me down now, so I can go see my baby?" Giggling at her trying to squirm out of my embrace, I let her down, and she rushed over to the baby. I watched the both of them dote on Kenzie and felt like the family was whole again. Taking a seat across from the triplets, I captured the moment on my phone.

"Bre'Ann, it's time for your nap, baby girl." Ant let her know, and she pouted.

"Ahh, Daddy, sissy and Kris just got here. Five more minutes please," she begged with her hands folded.

"Nah, lil' girl, you won't get me today. Kris will be here when you get up." He spoke without consulting me. I didn't plan on staying, and he knew what he was doing by putting me out there. Turning to me for confirmation, I had no choice but to say yes. I smiled when she ran off, knowing she would take one of the quickest naps in the history of naps. "How you feeling?" he asked once she was gone.

"I'm good. I was able to get a full night's rest which was good. How bout you?"

He sighed, cradling Kenzie in his arms before answering. "I'm straight. Glad to have my little one back. Feels good that we can just live life now that Kane is a dead issue. Literally." I nodded. "Now, I just need to make sure we good."

"We're good," I responded with all sincerity.

"You sure about that?" he pried, looking for more answers.

"I'm sure."

"So, since you're sure, when are you and my daughter coming back home?" I was left to face the elephant in the room that I planned on ignoring once I got there.

"I can't give you that answer right now," I said with uncertainty. What I really wanted to say was, *I'm ready to be home now, but I'm scared.*

"See, that only tells me that we're not on the same page, Ma. And we can't have that kind of discord between us." Ooh, he always had some smooth shit to say. "Let me go put Kenzie down then we can really talk." And I knew then what us "talking" would lead to.

My clit was already throbbing in my panties. I missed him; she missed him. I sat crossing and uncrossing my legs, waiting on his return. I was ready to argue my point about not coming back to stay for a little while just to distract myself from how horny I was. Getting up, I headed for the kitchen to fix something to eat for when Bre woke up. I decided to whip up a pan of baked ziti. It was one of her favorite meals.

"Don't you know as soon as I went to go put that little girl down, she started fussing."

I giggled because Kenzie was famous for that. "You and my dad are to blame for that. She's getting spoiled." I moved about the kitchen, chopping peppers and preparing the ground turkey.

"I'm sorry you walked in on the conversation with me and Maine. I needed someone to blame for Bre being taken, and I felt like you were that person at that time. I want you to know that I don't regret meeting or pursuing you. I was talking out of hurt and anger."

I turned the fire down low on the meat and turned around to face him. "I understand that you were coming from a hurt place, Ant. I do. My issue is you not allowing me to be there with you in the capacity that I was willing to. You basically shut me out, and I felt like I was beating myself up enough for both of us. Trust me, I tried to take things easy with you in the beginning because I had many run ins with Kane before you and I even became an item. I could have never predicted that he would've became the loose cannon he was. There may be too much damage to jump back into being us at the moment. I don't wanna break up, but a break seems necessary."

"Necessary for who? Don't speak for me. I don't believe in breaks. When you finish cooking, we going in **our** room, so I can make love to **my** pussy. Then, we gon' give **our** kids a bath and have movie night. It's real simple, Ma." He got up and tapped the table like our meeting was adjourned. "You need help with anything?" I was so turned on by his demeanor. I may have had on a game face, but my body had most certainly failed me. I turned the stove off completely.

"You think we can do that making love part now?" I licked my lips and smirked.

"It's your world, Ma. Whatever you want." I grabbed his hand and led him upstairs to **our** room. Peeling out of my jeans, I pulled my wool sweater over my head.

This would be the first time we had sex since Kenzie, so I knew he was about to fuck my soul into the corner. His eyes stalked me as he pulled his shirt over his head, showing his abs and v line. Ant's body was a work of art. My nigga was cut the fuck up and hung like a donkey. I bit my bottom lip, closing the space between us, and wrapped my arms around his neck, pressing my breasts against his bare chest. I snaked my tongue along the nape of his neck while he grabbed hold of my ample ass.

His touch felt different than the times before. He caressed my back in such a soothing way that turned me on even more, and it made me hornier. I pulled my lips from his neck and moved to his lips. I licked them before sucking on the bottom one.

"Mmmm," I moaned when he stuck his tongue in my mouth. I sucked on it and used one hand to massage the back of his neck and the other to play with his dick through his shorts. "I wanna feel you." I spoke into his mouth. In five seconds flat, his shorts were down, and he lifted me up and found his way into my wetness. "Ughhh."

He released a sigh and buried his head into my neck. The feeling of gratification was mutual between the two of us. My pussy was glad to receive him. He held my legs up, lifting me a little, and slowly stroked my middle so good I threw my head back. It didn't make any sense how he always made it a point to hit spots that were unknown.

"I love you so fuckin' much, Kristen. A nigga gon' make sure to always love you the right way," he declared with much conviction while looking at me through low eyes.

"I... love... you... too... baby." I broke up my words as I threw my pussy on his dick like I was trying to prove a point. He must've caught on as well because he put my back against the wall and tried to rearrange my uterus.

"Arghhhh," he growled, putting his hand around my neck and squeezing hard enough for me to gush.

"Oohh, fuckkkk!" I cried out as my clit thumped, and I rained on his shaft while he kept pumping into me.

He grunted a few minutes after me and released his seeds into my love canal. That one round had me spent, and I didn't have too much time to relish in the moment, not with Bre'Ann and Mackenzie Brown around. He carried me to the bathroom where I sucked him up until I felt like I was on the brink of lock jaw. I guess you could say that we made up because I didn't return back to my parents' house that night.

THE AFTERMATH
ONE MONTH LATER

<u>Chloe</u>

"Your Honor, my client is willing to sign off on joint custody with Mr. Brown, but in no way is she willing to give full custody." My lawyer spoke on my behalf. I looked over at Antwon and couldn't believe we were in court for the third time this month — all because he wouldn't budge on wanting full custody of Bre. And like him, I wasn't willing to give in either. My daughter deserved to be around me just as much as she was able to be around him and that bitch, Kristen.

I should've been in court for suing her for how she jumped on me. Two weeks after Bre and I returned home, Ant came by my house, instead of his lawyer, with the custody papers for me to sign. He had brought Kristen along, and as soon as I stepped out into the hallway, she was on me. I held my own this time, but because she caught me off guard, she got the best of me. I still refused to fill out the paperwork and told him to kiss my ass. Now here we were in court again.

"Your Honor, Ms. Reed has put herself in some sticky situations that would make anyone question her judgement," Ant's snazzy suit wearing ass lawyer said as he stood up and spoke to the judge. "In no way has my client called into question her love for Bre'Ann. It's her well-being while in Ms. Reed's care that is the problem at hand."

I wanted so badly to jump up and blurt out all the drugs that I knew for a fact that Ant had pushed up and down the interstate in the past that helped him fund his little music career. The only reason I didn't was because he hadn't mentioned the fact that I had kidnapped Bre and caused the both of us to be kidnapped by Kane's crazy ass. When he dropped me home the night he rescued us, I crumbled to the floor right in front of my door and cried silently. I cried because Maine made me watch him riddle Kane's body with bullets before turning to me and placing the smoking gun against my temple. He cursed the day that I ever entered his brother's life. I saw my life flash before my eyes as he pulled the trigger, and I heard the gun click. After promising to kill me if we had to meet under the same circumstances, he walked out.

That nightmare was over, and now here I was, entering a

new one. My eyes met Ant's as both of our lawyers argued our points. He held no sympathy for me whatsoever.

I wished now more than ever that I wouldn't have let my emotions get the best of me. Looking past him, I saw Kristen sitting behind him, holding their daughter. I hated that bitch. I hated her for the spell she had casted on both Kane and Ant. Kane had killed for the love of her. I was still stunned that he actually admitted to killing China.

I thought back to one of his high moments during our stay at the motel.

"I'm not a monster you know," he expressed as he sat at the table, wiping his nose after the hit he had. I sat across from him with my arms folded, watching him and peeking in on Bre as she slept.

"I can't tell. You're holding me and my daughter hostage, did the same with your ex, and let's not forget that you're a murderer. I think the title monster fits you quite well."

"I didn't mean to kill her. She was plotting on me with Kristen. When I found the texts in her phone, I blacked out and just couldn't stop hitting her." I did my best not to portray how I felt in order to keep him talking. "I don't know how to tell her mother that her daughter won't have a proper funeral. We buried her in the cemetery near my house."

He had started to nod off, but I needed the rest of the informa-tion. I wanted to know where Chloe's body was. We never got along, but she had a child, a family that I was sure was looking for her. I would want someone to do the same for me.

"Who's we?" I pried.

"Me and my cousin, Simone." I swallowed hard and got up from the table.

A couple days after being back home, I took it upon myself to go to the police station and report what Kane had told me. When they inquired about his whereabouts, I let them know that I hadn't heard from him since finding out the information. I remembered Simone's name because he had mentioned his cousin being a singer. I couldn't understand why she would risk her career and her freedom for his crazy ass. By the cop's response, I couldn't gauge whether he believed me or not. I felt better about reporting it though. I had been so zoned out that I didn't hear the judge bang her gavel twice.

"I've had enough of listening to the two of you." She motioned to both my lawyer and Ant's. "I would like to hear from the parents now. Please, Ms. Reed, stand where you are and tell me why we are here for the third hearing."

"Your Honor, I have tried on multiple occasions to speak with Antwon about joint custody, but we've gotten nowhere. He's cut all communication with me, forcing me to deal with his lawyer. I love my daughter, and she should be raised with her biological mother."

"Are you working right now, Ms. Reed?"

"I'll be returning to work next week at a law firm." That wasn't a complete lie. I did, in fact, reach out to my old boss about getting my job back after he let me go. The last time we spoke, he said he'd consider it, and I'd be on probation. That wasn't a problem for me. I was back in the right state of mind to do my job. Money wasn't an issue though. I had always been a saver, so I had a nice little nest egg set aside.

"Okay, Ms. Reed, you may be seated. Mr. Brown, would you stand and address the court?"

"Your Honor, like my lawyer previously stated, in no way am I saying that Ms. Reed doesn't love our daughter. I want them to maintain a relationship, but I want my daughter to be with me solely. I'm willing to set up a visitation schedule."

The judge sat back and crossed her arms, looking at him with questioning eyes. "Do you mind telling me what events led up to the discord between the two of you that makes you think you feel that sole custody should be awarded to you?"

I looked forward, attempting to meet his eyes. There was no way around the question, and I knew that it was over for me.

"She tried to kidnap her on a supervised visit. I had to remove Bre'Ann from her mother's care because of an unsafe relationship she was in." I could tell he didn't want to divulge that information, but I also knew he wasn't going to lie.

"Thank you, Mr. Brown. We're going to recess for now, and I'll be back with my decision within the next hour." She banged her gavel and walked to the back. My head dropped, and I did my best to withhold the tears. I didn't want to throw in the towel, but what the hell else could I do?

"Chloe, I have to be honest with you. We're doing the best

we can, but the kidnapping may do us in." My lawyer let me know with less than hopeful eyes.

"Do ya fucking job and figure it out!" I snapped at him before powerwalking out behind Ant and Kristen. "You're really a fucking piece of work, you know that!" I shouted behind their backs. "Y'all have your own child. Why you wanna play family with mine?"

Kristen turned quickly and stormed over to me, leaving Ant waiting for her. "And you think running after us is going to help your case? You look crazy. Get yourself together and give him something to respect again and maybe things will start to work in your favor. I love Bre'Ann to life, and you're absolutely right that he and I have our own child that we share. The fact still remains that I look at your daughter as mine. Stop forgetting that your actions are the reason we're here in the first place. Don't make me forget where we are physically and tag that ass again."

"All rise," the bailiff said as we reentered the court room. It was the quickest hour of my life.

"You may be seated. I'm going to do something unorthodox today. Can I just have the parents stand only?" Both Ant and I stood. "I've heard both arguments over the last few hearings, and what I can say is that the both of you have proven that your daughter is the center of both of your worlds. Usually in custody cases, judges' side with the mom unless they can be proven completely unfit. In this case, Ms. Reed is not an unfit parent. I have, however, taken into account the decisions that have led you both before me. With that being said, I'm awarding sole custody to Mr. Brown." I hung my head, and all I could do was cry. The decision was a dagger to my heart. "Ms. Reed, I'm awarding you visitation that I'm giving the two of you one week to figure out amongst yourselves and have an agreement presented to the court by your lawyers. Court's adjourned."

She banged the gavel again, and I walked out without saying anything to my lawyer. There was nothing left to say. I had done all I could. I wasn't sure what kind of world we lived in now where the father had more rights than a mother.

"Chloe." I heard my name called and turned to find Ant jogging down the court steps. I didn't have the energy to sit here and have him rub the verdict in my face. I kept it moving onto the street and to my car. "Chloe, man, wait up." He caught up to me and grabbed at my arm. "Every other weekend and every other holiday."

"What?"

"The visitation agreement. Every other weekend and every other holiday, cool?"

With no other choice, I agreed. "Cool." I went to walk away, and he grabbed at my hand again. On the outside, you'd think we were having a friendly exchange with the handshake, but the pressure he put on my hand was anything but friendly. "I had to go about this the right way, but you're fresh out of chances with me. If you try to pull another stunt, I'm going to put a bullet here and here." He pointed to my forehead and my heart. "Smile if you understand."

Smiling, I nodded. He did the same before turning away and walking off. I watched as Kristen descended the steps with her daughter strapped to her chest, and Ant held out his hand for her to take. And just like that, the bitch had won again.

SIMONE

Maine meant what he said when he told me to consider my contract null and void. Like a fool, I went up to the studio a week after the hotel debacle and was handed my last royalty check, along with a note that let me know in not too many words not to expect anything else. I was then escorted off the property by security. My life was in shambles again. The only thing I could say I had done right was putting aside a little money for myself in case of emergencies. Only this wasn't an emergency. The plug had literally been pulled on my career.

The press had gotten hold of my release from my contract and had a field day with it. The headlines read *Songstress Simone B. suddenly dropped from her label.* I had been cooped up in the house since then. My phone was turned off, and I'd shut myself off from the world. The most I did was shower, eat here and there, and write music. I hadn't heard anything from Kane, and I was happy about it. I had a feeling that he was no longer amongst the living, and family or not, I couldn't say that I was sad about it.

I'd retreated back to my apartment after being holed up in the hotel, healing from the beating I took. Kaia packed a mean punch, and I didn't have any ill feelings toward her for whipping my ass. I only wished that this whole thing didn't end the friendship I had with Maine. I thought of him often and wondered how he was. I mean, yeah, I could've turned on the TV and gotten an update, but I missed talking to him.

Crawling out the bed, I headed to the fridge to make myself a cobb salad. I had been surviving on salads and endless bottles of Moscato. I no longer wanted to feel sorry for myself, but what else could I do? Seeing that there was no eggs to complete the salad, I threw my head back in annoyance. My fridge had seen better days, and now I was forced to go out to the market for a quick food haul.

Winter was upon us, and today was one of those cold ass days. I threw on a pair of Nike sweats, a hoodie, and my Ugg boots. My Gucci puffer coat would fight against the frigid weather outside. I grabbed my phone and turned it on for the first time in a while. As soon as it powered up, a stream of messages and missed calls popped up on the screen. I disregarded them, threw my hoodie over my head, and kept it pushing.

"Bitch, ain't that Simone B. from Promise Records over

there in the Gucci bubble?" I heard a female say as I pushed my cart through the dairy aisle in Whole Foods.

"You mean was?" The girl corrected. I kept moving as if I couldn't hear them. I was already embarrassed enough. I had gone from being on top to being just a regular female that other females talked about. "I heard that she was sleeping with one of them niggas on the label, and the girl found out what was going on and had to tap that ass." Oh, see, now she had gone too far.

"Umm, excuse me, who is your source?"

"My source?" She countered with a stank look.

"Yes, your source, boo. You out here throwing dirt on my name, so I'm hoping that your info is from a credible source." She rolled her eyes and sucked her teeth but had no response. "That's exactly what I thought. Fact check before you talk shit, bitch. And while you're out here worrying about what I did or didn't do, worry about that track that's playing peek a boo in front of your leave out, sis." Pushing my cart, I picked up the rest of my items and went to check out.

I had enough food to last me a little while. That was a good thing because after that bullshit, I was crawling back into my hole. I put my salad together and went to sit at my desk where my keyboard was set up. I knew after consuming some food, I would have the energy to write. My phone rang, and I let it go to voicemail while I continued to eat. Once I was good and full, I wrote a hook and had a chorus done in under an hour.

Writing was my way of venting and keeping from harming myself. I felt like it was the only thing that was keeping me alive at this point. While working on the verses, I unlocked my phone to see if I could pull from anything that I had written in my notes over the past year. A voicemail notification from the last number that had called twenty minutes ago popped up on the screen. I didn't know why, but something was saying that I needed to listen to the message, so I did.

"Hello, Ms. Batista, this is Detective Raymond down at the twenty-first precinct. I've been trying to get a hold of you for some time now regarding an urgent matter. If you can give me a call back at 917-428-9078 as soon as possible, that would be great. Thank you." The message ended, and my heart raced. My palms got sweaty, and my throat felt like sandpaper. Why would a detective be reaching out to me if he didn't already know something?

"Shit, shit, shit," I said aloud as I paced the floor with my phone clutched in my hand, thinking about whether or not I should call him back. I could always pretend I didn't see the call, but that would only make him think I was avoiding him. I went to check my other messages and scanned through to see that the same number had left a message three times before. With shaky hands, I pressed the option on my iPhone to dial the number back.

It rang three times, and that was good enough for me to say I called. I went to hang up, and the call connected. **"Detective Raymond, how can I help you?"**

"Uh." My words got stuck in my throat. **"Umm, my name is Simone Batista. I received a message from you today, and I'm returning your call."** I hoped that this was the one time that I was confused with the other Batistas in the city.

"Oh, yes, Ms. Batista. Do you mind if I call you Simone?"

"No, that's fine."

"Great. Well, I'm reaching out regarding the death of China Torres. Do you have some time to come down to the station and answer some questions?"

"Umm, yeah, sure thing," I replied, my voice cracking.

"Okay, it's the twenty-first precinct in White Plains. I can send you the address if you need directions."

"No need. I'll Google Map it. Thank you."

"Sure thing. When you get here, ask for Detective Raymond, and I'll come right out front to get you." I hung up the phone and said a quick prayer up to God to forgive me for my sins.

At the police station, I asked for the detective and waited on pins and needles for him to come up front. When he did, I was taken aback by how strikingly handsome he was. I didn't have time to live in that moment of admiring him though because once he said follow me, I felt like I was walking the green mile.

"Have a seat and I'm going to go get a woman so that you feel more comfortable."

"Thank you, but that won't be necessary." I appreciated the gesture, but the only thing that he could do right now to make me feel more comfortable was to let me walk my ass back up out of here.

"Okay, well, let's get started then." He sat back down and placed a file on the desk. "How did you know the victim?"

"She and my cousin, Kane, share a child. I can't say that I really knew her." I prayed that me not knowing China well would help me in some way.

"And do you happen to know the whereabouts of your cousin, Kane? I've been trying to reach out to him as well."

"I haven't spoken to Kane in over a month. It's not uncommon for him to go MIA sometimes."

"Do you know if he's aware of his child's mother's death?"

"I can't be too sure. As I said, it's been a while since we've spoken." I started to fidget in my chair, and my underarms became sweaty. I wanted him to get to the point of why I was here, but I didn't want to push him.

"Hmm, odd but okay. Look at this picture and tell me what you see." He opened the folder and showed a picture of the shallow grave Kane and I had dug up along with the garbage bags we put China in. I couldn't hold back my tears.

"I would show you what we found in those bags, but the body was badly decomposed. Can I tell you something that happened about a month ago?" I nodded my head yes as I tried to get myself together, but the tears wouldn't stop falling.

"A woman by the name of Chloe Reed came into the station to report a murder. According to her, her boyfriend, Kane, had confessed to said murder and told her where the body was. He also went on to tell her that he had help from his cousin, Simone, to get rid of this body. So, now that you know exactly why we're here, Ms. Batista, I need you to help me help you."

The flood gates opened. I told him everything about what happened to China and how I became an accomplice after being threatened by Kane. By the time I was finished, I was crying so hard that my body started to shake. This was no longer about Kane but about how I had ruined my life by allowing him to have power over me as he had done with many of his women.

"Simone Batista, you are under arrest for the murder of China Torres. You have the right to remain silent..." I didn't hear anything else he said as I closed my eyes and tuned everything out around me.

MAINE

"Thank you for coming out to fuck with me, L.A. The love is definitely real. Until next time, peace." The high that I had on stage slowly died once I walked off and was met backstage by Playboy and Ant. The face I really wanted to see was my girl's — if I could even still call her that. Kaia still wasn't fucking with me after that run in she had with Simone.

I tried in so many different ways to say sorry, down to getting creative and having the apology written in the sky. She still wasn't budging for shit. She was making a nigga feel it for sure.

"Bro, you gotta change your attitude. You fucking up the mood. You got a club appearance to go to after this," Ant coached, and I gave him a look that said *get the fuck on*. "I don't give a damn about that look, my nigga. Kaia gon' come around. You just gotta give her some time."

"That's easy for you to say. You and Kristen are together and on good terms." I didn't want to hear nothing about Kaia coming around eventually. I needed us on the same page like yesterday.

"Yoo, y'all seen this shit on TMZ today?" Play asked dramatically, passing his phone to Ant. Ant shook his head and passed the phone to me.

Former up-and-coming R&B sensation, Simone B, charged with first degree murder. Singer arrested and held without bail. Shrugging my shoulders, I handed the phone back to Play. I knew it was coming at any point. Although it was fucked up how she was involved with trying to take us down, it was even more fucked up that she was going down for a murder Kane committed. Karma ain't no hoe.

"That shit crazy. Maybe that's why they were tryna reach out for a comment. It's good they got to her before I did. I had plans to do her real dirty," Ant stated while texting on his phone. I checked my own phone and saw a couple messages but saw none from Kaia, so I shoved it back in my pocket.

"Bro, you gotta cancel that whole club appearance shit. I need to get to the home front. This shit with Kaia gotta end tonight." I was done trying to be understanding of how she felt. Her ass was going to hear me out.

"Aight. You catching a red eye?"

"Yep. I'll hit you when I touch down."

I dapped him and Play up and headed out. I knew Kaia was at my house with the kids because I could see her asleep in my bed through the app I had on my phone. She slept with both Chase and Kymani in the bed. Her arm was draped across the both of them protectively. I was surprised to see her there since she'd called herself moving back in with her parents. I missed my girl, and I was still willing to move Heaven and Earth to get her back.

Arriving home, I did my best to walk through the house without waking up the kids. Entering the bedroom, I tried to move them from under Kaia's arm quietly but failed and ended up waking her. Her eyes shot open, and she sat up a little. Seeing that it was me, she released her grip and allowed me to take the kids to their bedroom. When I returned, she had her back facing the door.

"Kaia," I called out to her, and she ignored me. I knew she was being stubborn. I already had her in the bed, and if everything went my way, she wouldn't leave. I said nothing as I stripped out of my clothes down to my boxers.

I slid in bed behind her and pulled her into my arms. Her body tensed up, but I had something for that. I pulled up her nightgown to find that she had no panties on. Sliding under the covers, I opened her legs with little to no effort and licked her slit. She spread her legs a little wider like she knew what it was I was going to do next. I used my fingers to open up her pussy lips and sucked on her clit, making her release the sexiest moan. I kept at it, applying enough pressure to her clit that it started to swell in my mouth. The scent of her made me go harder.

"Ugh, shit," she cried out softly. Moving at her own rhythm, I knew she was about to reach her peak. I stuck my finger in her wet box to get her there faster. "Yeah, yeah." She sounded like one of those girls in the porn videos as she thrusted back and forth on my finger. I moved my tongue and gave her pussy two soft slaps, and she came for me like I knew she would.

Thinking I was done, she sucked in her bottom lip and closed her legs tightly to savor the feeling of the orgasm. Positioning myself behind her, I lifted her leg slightly in the scissor position and slid my dick into her tight box. She gripped me like the warmest hug, holding my dick hostage.

"Ssss," she hissed as I gave her all nine inches of hard dick. I was hitting her so good that it felt like I was making up for lost time. Since she wasn't accepting my verbal apology, I was hoping that the dick down would put us on the same page again.

"Arghhh," I growled while biting on her neck. She had started to squeeze her pussy muscles again, and I gripped her waist tightly. *Basketball, soccer, football.* I thought about sports in my head to keep from bussin' before her. "Stop doing that shit, Kaia." I slapped her ass, and it jiggled.

I could feel her walls contracting as she came, and I wasn't too far behind her, filling her with my seeds. This was my happy place — inside her. She didn't give me a chance to savor the moment this time. Peeling away from my semi hard dick, she stood up.

"Thanks. Can you get up, so I change the sheets and put my babies back in bed?" Her tone was cold, and for the first time since we'd been together, I felt a mental distance between us. The feeling was not a good one. I watched as she casually sauntered off into the bathroom. Sitting up in the bed, I waited for her to return, my dick still covered in her essence. I wasn't going another night with us being on bad terms.

She returned with a new set of sheets in hand. I wasn't budging. For a couple seconds, we stared at each other, both trying to figure out our next move. Huffing, she threw the sheets at me and stormed back into the bathroom. This time, she slammed the door behind her.

"Can you just go somewhere, Maine? Damn." She spoke through the door, sounding aggravated as hell. I couldn't help but laugh. Putting my boxers back on, I went over and leaned up against the bathroom door.

"You and I both know I ain't going nowhere, shorty. We can either talk through this door or you can come out. Either way, we gotta talk, Ma." She didn't respond. "Cool, I'll go first. Kaia, you know I'd never do anything to intentionally hurt you or make you feel like I don't value what you mean to me. Me befriending Simone in no way had anything to do with my love for you, bae. I made a stupid decision, and I'm sorry for that. I swear on our kids that nothing happened between us. That crazy girl roofied my stupid ass."

I put my head up against the door, waiting for her to say something. Silence wasn't a good sign. I was prepared for her to scream, fight, or curse me out. I needed something besides silence. The door opened suddenly, and I stumbled forward.

"First of all, I already know that nothing happened. If it did, yo' ass wouldn't be alive to tell the story. And I'm aware that you value me as your woman. The problem is you don't respect my mind." She moved around me and began pulling the sheets off the bed.

"What you mean?"

She stopped pulling at the sheets and gave me her full attention. "I'm saying when I told you something was off about Simone, you should've caught on then. Not you though. You wanted to do ya own thing and keep the lines of communication open. How we supposed to be a team if you don't let me guard you? You were steady playing defense."

"Okay, now you lost me. Your analogies are all over the place, shorty." She hit me with the sheet, and I saw a trace of a smirk on her face.

"Shut up. You know what I mean." I grabbed her by the arm and pulled her into my chest.

"No, I know what you said. Tryna sound all deep and shit. You know I love you, right?" I went to kiss her lips, and she dodged it, giving me her cheek.

"Nah, I'm just playing." She giggled. "I love you too, and I accept your apology." Finally after a whole damn month, I wanted to say, but I didn't. She forgave me, and that was all that mattered. "I meant to ask you, have you heard anything from Kandice's mother or from that detective?"

"Nope." When she sent me the video of Kandice's mother trying to blackmail me, all I could do was laugh. If she thought she was getting a hundred thousand dollars from me, she was smoking laced blunts or something. I could've sent her to where her daughter currently resided since she claimed she wanted to find her so bad, but I came up with a better idea. I sent the video straight to my lawyer and let him handle it.

"Babe."

"Hmm?"

"I think we have time to go again." Her eyes twinkled. My little freak.

"Oh, ya coochie don't hurt?"

"It's a little sore. Nothing that a little tongue action can't fix." I was more than willing to oblige. I went from the guy that didn't show love to women to picking the right one to give all my love to. And I wouldn't have it any other way.

KAIA

"Happy birthday, fat man," I squealed in Chase's ear, waking him up from his sleep. Today was his first birthday, and we had so much planned. There were back-to-back celebrations within this last month alone. Shanice and I had been accepted into business school, Kristen had opened up a new salon that Heaven was now running, and my baby was on the Hot Billboard 100's. Life was good, and it felt even better.

"Dada," Chase said clearer than any other words he was learning daily. He loved him some Maine. And you couldn't tell Maine nothing about his lil' man.

"Come on, fat man. Let's get you ready for the day, then we can go wake your little spoiled sister up."

He giggled and clapped once his little feet hit the floor. Chase had completely skipped the walking stage and went straight to running with his little bowlegged self. I helped him up on his stepping stool to brush the few teeth he had and wash his little face before setting up the tub for him.

Watching him splash around in the water, I couldn't believe how life had turned out. Here I was, mothering the child of my enemy, and I didn't have any malice in my heart whatsoever. And I didn't just love him because I loved Maine. My love came naturally for him, no different than what I felt for Kymani.

"Shorty, come get yo' shitty ass daughter. Look at this." Maine came barging in the bathroom with Mani outstretched in front of him.

I smelled her diaper before he even made it in front of me. I could see the pamper was full, and the poop was seeping out from the sides. I laughed so hard at Maine's facial expression. He was pissed off and about to be further pissed because he was changing that damn diaper.

"Oh, hell no. She can't be my daughter when she on shitty time. Go head and handle up on that. That changing table that you insisted on setting up in here is gon' come right in handy." I was convinced that Maine liked to buy baby stuff just to say he bought it. I didn't know who was worse, him or Ant. He huffed and talked shit under his breath, but he got to that changing table like I said. If I wasn't busy washing up Chase, I would've recorded his silly ass as he talked to Kymani about etiquette when he was around.

"Mani, baby girl, you know Daddy love you to the moon, but you really have to watch your diet. This pamper is way too heavy for a nine-month-old." It took him five minutes to change a diaper I would've had done in two. We got the kids ready and headed out the door to breakfast at Ma Jane's house where everybody else was. I had the day all planned out, even down to our outfits. We looked good as a unit. Ma Jane had a big spread of every breakfast item that your heart desired when we walked in.

"Ma Jane, you do know that it's just the immediate family that's gonna be here, right? And Chase is only one."

"And you do know that I will cuss you out and tell you I love you in the same breath, right?" I clamped my lips shut and turned to back out of her kitchen. "Alright now, love you, baby." That lady was a trip. Bump that, she was a whole vacation. I went back to rejoin the family in the dining room and sat next to Maine. Both Chase and Kymani were in their highchairs near my mom, and Kenzie was in Ant's lap where she always was.

Clink clink. Ant tapped his glass with his fork as he stood up to speak.

"Family, can I have your attention please?" We all stopped our side chatter and gave him our attention. "I first wanna start by saying happy birthday to my nephew. Chase, we love you, and when you get old enough, you know there's a spot on the throne for you at Promise Records. Second, I wanna tell each and every one of you that I love y'all, even you, Heaven." We all burst out laughing, and Heaven flipped him off.

"Oooh, Auntie Heaven, that's bad," Bre cut in, slapping her own hand like she was reprimanding Heaven.

"Auntie sorry, boo. Go head, Ant." She stuck her tongue out at him, and he smiled.

"Yeah, so, we been through some trials, man, within the past year and a half. Most of which we came out on the winning end of and others not so much." I felt a cry building up in me thinking about Mecca. I missed my best friend dearly. I knew it wasn't just by happen stance that we were able to rid ourselves of Kane. My girl was with us every step of the way. "I want y'all to know that we gon' remain grounded, keep rocking, and keep getting to this money."

"Man, sit yo' A-S-S down. You went from a heartwarming family speech to a speech you would give at one of the record label meetings in all of five seconds," Play joked, and we howled in laughter. This was what it was all about. Finding a love that you couldn't ignore and creating something so beautiful that everyone around you felt it. This was my hood love story, and it felt damn good to get my happy ending.

THE END

Did you enjoy the read?
Let us know how much by leaving us a review on Amazon
and Goodreads.

OTHER BOOKS BY

<u>URBAN AINT DEAD</u>

Tales 4rm Da Dale

The Hottest Summer Ever

Hittin' Licks For The Holidays: Atlanta

Wet Dreams On Lockdown: The Nurse

By **Elijah R. Freeman**

Despite The Odds

By **Juhnell Morgan**

Good Girl Gone Rogue

By **Manny Black**

Hittaz

Hittaz 2

Hittaz 3

Hittaz 4

Coldhearted

By **Lou Garden Price, Sr.**

Charge It To The Game

Charge It To The Game 2

A Summer To Remember With My Hitta

Snatched Up By A Hitta

Santa Sent Me A Real One For Christmas

Wet Dreams on Lockdown: The Unit Manager

Thug Me The Right Way 2

By **Nai**

A Setup For Revenge

Wet Dreams On Lockdown: The Librarian

By **Ashley Williams**

Ridin' For You

Trickin' on a Heaux for Christmas: A BBW Love Story

Homie Hoppin' For The Holidays

Wet Dreams on Lockdown: The Female C.O

By **Telia Teanna**

The State's Witness

The State's Witness 2

The State's Witness 3

This Time Won't You Save Me

By **Kyiris Ashley**

Stuck In The Trenches

Stuck In The Trenches 2

By **Huff Tha Great**

The Swipe

By **Toōla**

Melted the Heart of a Menace

Wet Dreams On Lockdown: Lieutenant Grace

By P. Wise

Merry Trapmas: Ice & Frost

By **Mia Sky**

Thug Me The Right Way

By **DiamondATL & Nai**

Wet Dreams on Lockdown: The Male C.O

By **Tamyra Griffin**

Wet Dreams On Lockdown: The Counselor

By **Paris Iman**

Wet Dreams On Lockdown: The Warden

By **Shawnice**

Wet Dreams On Lockdown: The Captain

By **TN Jones**

COMING SOON FROM

<u>URBAN AINT DEAD</u>

How To Publish A Book From Prison
The Hottest Summer Ever 2
THE G-CODE
Tales 4rm Da Dale 2
By **Elijah R. Freeman**

Hittaz 5
Coldhearted 2
By **Lou Garden Price, Sr.**

The Swipe 2
By **Toola**

Good Girl Gone Rogue 2
By **Manny Black**

Despite The Odds 2
Hittin' Licks For The Holidays: Chicago
By **Juhnell Morgan**

Charge It To The Game 3
By **Nai**

A Setup For Revenge 2
By **Ashley Williams**

This Time Won't You Save Me 2
By **Kyiris Ashley**

Ridin' Forever
By **Telia Teanna**

A Gangsta's Last Kiss
By **Mia Sky**

Pretti & The Beast
By **P. Wise**

Atlantastan
By **Chris Green**

STAY CONNECTED

Follow
Elijah R. Freeman
On Social Media
FB: Elijah R. Freeman
IG: @the_future_of_urban_fiction